THE HOUSE ON THE HILL

Rebecca, The House On The Hill

JACQUELINE MAURICE

authorHOUSE®

AuthorHouse™ UK
1663 Liberty Drive
Bloomington, IN 47403 USA
www.authorhouse.co.uk
Phone: 0800.197.4150

Published by AuthorHouse 11/17/2016

ISBN: 978-1-5246-6462-6 (sc)
ISBN: 978-1-5246-6461-9 (e)

Print information available on the last page.

This book is printed on acid-free paper.

To Mrs Spokes and my school friends at Pond House, Sally for her long-term friendship, James for his patience and Aunt Gina for her encouragement.

Jacqueline Maurice

Chapter 1

SHE HAD KEPT the secret for so many years. She had never told anyone until now. It had been a painful decision, but at the time, it had seemed the only solution, the kindest, hardest and loneliest.

She had never considered herself to be brave. Of course she had feelings. Every single nerve ending in her body bore witness to that. But those around her never noticed. How could they? They were all too preoccupied with their own private little worlds. And she didn't have a world. She was, in their eyes, a fitment, a thing, part of the furniture, devoid of all feelings.

A faint smile touched her violet eyes and a warm glow brushed her cheeks accentuating the rich auburn of her thick, short wavy hair with its intermittent streaks of grey. Fine lines caressed her face as if daring her to smile. How time had changed her! Where was the person she once was, so full of life's expectancies and promises.

She was a proud woman, tall, erect, a pillar of discretion exuding a confidence which some may have found intimidating. But when her full mouth creased and her eyes danced with warmth, she was more than touchable. She was a long lost Mother, a friend, bosom of many a child's longing.

Rebecca watched her Aunt apprehensively. They had always been very, very close and she had sensed for a long while that there was something hidden away in the dark recesses of time. What it could possibly be she had no idea. Instinctively she felt it was not a figment of her imagination, not after all these years.

'Aunt Anne, can I make you a hot drink?' she asked hesitantly. 'Don't fuss' came the curt reply. 'Molly will be here shortly. There's no need for you to be messing around in the kitchen!' Rebecca sighed. Her Aunt had always been stubbornly single minded and even now with her leg strapped after falling on a slippery pavement her character had not changed to accommodate her, albeit temporary, disability. But despite her Aunt's seemingly unyielding disposition, she adored her and could not bear to think of her suffering in the slightest way. How different if Mother could have been so unselfish and caring. But sisters were never alike and since her Mother had been laid to rest, she had come to depend and draw on her Aunt's love even more. It was Aunt Anne who was always ready with a smile or word of encouragement when she needed, even when her Mother was alive.

Rebecca's Aunt regarded her niece beneath lowered lids. She studied her every facial feature and each nervous little gesture. Her sister's face mirrored in her mind's eye. How beautiful she was with her pale, unflawed skin, deep blue eyes and the rich auburn hair which had been inherited as a family heirloom. A strong determined jawline was the only recognition to her Father. Her so called Father! Anne sighed. What a brutish, selfish man he had turned out to be. Fortunately he was unable to extricate the family money in the few years he was around. Rebecca's recollections of him were vague. 'Better that way' Anne had always told her sister. 'Good riddance and all that!'

Rebecca looked at her Aunt quizzically. 'What were you thinking about?' she asked. 'Just reminiscing my dear, just reminiscing.'

Chapter 2

SHE HAD BEEN a young girl when she had met Sam, younger than Rebecca was now but in those days so much younger in every possible way. She had never known the freedom that Rebecca enjoyed, never had the boyfriends taking her to balls and the thrill of dressing up in beautiful long, silk dresses and feeling pretty and admired. No, her parents would never have allowed anything like that. She was just plain Anne until Sam came along. But she could never take him home. Sam was only the local boy whose family's status did not match their own by any stretch of the imagination. Her sister's beaus were always from the elite. Well, that's how the family always described them. 'Why don't you find yourself a good looking young man like your sister' the family would jibe. 'Leave me alone' she would retort, 'I can't stand those pompous, self-opinionated creatures.' But deep down it hurt. Hurt so badly that she feared the wounds would open up revealing to everyone the pain and misery she was feeling inside.

But then along came Sam. He was the son of the newsagent in the village and riding by on his polished bicycle with a knowing twinkle in his eye, he saw in Anne the most beautiful girl he had ever seen. 'Ma, she's like a flower!' he would gush enthusiastically. His Mother would look at him, her mouth wide open in amazement. 'And what would you be saying about them posh folks up the hill? She's not for you son. She be one of the gentry!' 'Gentry or no gentry, she smiles at me Ma. I know that!' His Mother sighed in disbelief wondering about her son's total disregard for those above his station. But Sam was right. Anne always looked for him and a blush would colour her cheeks when he passed by giving her that knowing wink.

It was the year leading up to her sister's marriage that they had more opportunity to spend time together, in secret of course. For once everyone was too busy to chide or question her as to what she was doing. And for the first time she fell deeply and passionately in love.

If only the war hadn't interrupted our lives, Anne reflected sadly. If only! Sam was called up and her sister's husband followed soon after. But with all the turmoil there was still much rejoicing at home. 'Your sister's going to have a child' she was told. And then the rejoicing turned to shame. She was pregnant too!

Her Mother and Father kept the secret well. No-one saw her in the village and war brought other problems to occupy the many minds. They allowed her, grudgingly, to read Sam's letters but the telegram came as a shock, even for them. It wasn't long before they added that it was all for the best. 'You could never have married him' her Mother would say. 'We would never have allowed it!'

The two sisters with their simultaneous pregnancies didn't have much to say to one another. Not even after Sam's death. Anne felt her sister despised her for taking away so much of the family joy. But she was too full of grief and love for her unborn child to care about that.

It was ironical really, both sisters in labour at the same time. Anne could still picture the elderly midwife's face round, warm and caring. A face that had seen it all and borne all the miseries and happiness in her years.

'Your sister's broken water' she exclaimed. 'It won't be long now!' The midwife looked tired and sad on her return, small beads of perspiration covering her forehead and the darkish area of her upper lip. 'How is she?' Anne asked. The round warm, caring face tried hard to wear a smile. 'How's my sister?' Anne insisted. 'The baby's stillborn' the midwife replied. 'Your sister doesn't know. She's sound asleep, poor mite. A beautiful little girl she was too!' 'Have you told my parents?' Anne asked nervously. 'Not yet my lass, now don't you fret? Come on, push hard now! There's a life in you waiting to be born.'

Anne heard the shrill cry and through a haze watched the midwife busying herself cooing and clucking like an old Mother hen. 'Is my baby all right?' she cried. 'Is my baby all right?' 'Now, now' the soothing voice responded, 'you've a beautiful baby girl that God's given you, a beautiful wee bonnie girl.' Anne stared at the midwife. 'Please listen to me' she begged. 'Please listen to me!' The midwife hesitated, startled by the insistence in Anne's voice. 'I want you to let my sister have my child. I want you to tell her that my child was still born. Only you and I need ever know the truth!' The midwife did not try to conceal the shock that was now written across her pallid face. 'What nonsense are you talking! What nonsense indeed!' 'Please, Anne begged. 'My baby is born out of wedlock. My parents have already made plans that she should never inherit what is rightfully hers and she'll be sent away to people I will never know. I want to see my daughter grow, to have a beautiful home and be brought up with love. This way I can always watch over her!' She paused, tears streaming uncontrollably down her cheeks. 'I love her so much. I don't want to be parted from her. I loved her Father and he loved me!' The midwife nodded wearily, another sadness to lock away in her heavy heart. 'All right my lass' she whispered, 'all right, now don't you fret.'

Anne looked up at Rebecca sitting so poised, patiently sipping her tea. What a beautiful compassionate creature she had grown to be. Sam would have been proud of her; and the chin? Sam's chin, strong and defined. Not the weak chinless wonder of her so called Father.

'Rebecca' 'Yes' she replied eagerly. 'The family solicitor will be here in half an hour and I'd like to see him in private.' 'Is anything wrong?' Rebecca asked. 'No, no. Nothing's wrong. I've just something I have to tell him. Something I haven't told anyone all these years!' she added quietly, under her breath.

Chapter 3

'WILL YOU HAVE a cognac or whisky?' Anne asked. Charles beamed his normal ebullient smile. A cognac will do nicely thank you.' Having decided on a small sherry for herself, Anne settled in the large armchair at the same time resting her leg on the foot-stool facing Charles. 'I'm so pleased you could find time to come this afternoon' she smiled warmly. Charles nodded. He had known Anne since she was a child. Had watched her grow into a handsome striking woman and had often wondered why she had never married. His memory gently wandered back in time and he recalled how withdrawn she used to be, always overpowered by her elder sister Sarah. He had thought that she would change as she grew older and he had been right. There had been rumours a long time back that she had become smitten with a lad from the village but idle gossip was not an unusual feature of those days.

Charles' cheeks flushed slightly, warmed by the cognac which slowly trickled through his veins. His once thick black hair had gradually turned to a distinguished silvery grey and, as always, he was immaculately dressed, today in a light grey worsted suit, crisp white shirt with a silk maroon tie and handkerchief to match. Anne's parents, Jack and Mary Henderson, had brought their business to him when he needed to establish himself as a solicitor in Roynick. They were part of the land owning families in the area and their many friends soon took the gentle hints of Jack Henderson to bring their business to him. Their passing had been a sad affair, Jack suffering a heart attack and Mary losing her desire to live without him. Everyone understood. Her heart was too heavy with grief and less than a year later she had lost the will to live.

Sarah, the elder daughter, had been the apple of her Mother's eye. Mary could never understand Anne, nor did she really try to. Jack would encourage her to show their younger daughter more interest and affection but to no avail. As for himself, he adored Anne, but Sarah always had her way no matter what. It was a blessing, Charles often thought, that they were not around to witness the untimely death of their elder daughter.

Anne warmed to Charles Matthews as he sipped on his cognac. He was such a comfortable person to be with. She remembered him coming to the House on the Hill when she was young and being hastily ushered out of the room with her sister Sarah. The two girls were never privy to their conversation and she wondered what conspiracies they were involved in. He was such a mysterious young man. It was only as she grew older that she understood the nature of his calls.

His advice as the family solicitor was well respected and his clientele in Roynick expanded to such an extent that his partner and himself were never short of business, all with thanks to the complete trust of the Hendersons.

'I do appreciate your taking the time to call' Anne continued. 'You really must be very busy with your partner away!' 'Nothing that we can't manage' Charles gesticulated. 'Fortunately Gerald has joined us now.' Anne smiled. Gerald was so much like his Father and it was good that the business would continue with his heir. 'Yes, he's a good son with a good head on his shoulders. I feel now that all the work will not have been in vain.' Charles paused, reflecting how comfortable it was to be sitting chatting with a woman like Anne. Since the loss of his wife so much had changed. Sadness drifted across his face. 'How have you been coping?' Anne asked, sensing his change of mood. 'Not too badly. It takes time you know.' He paused, as if deep in thought. 'I'm sorry but sitting here with you brought back happy memories my dear.' Anne sighed. 'Charles' she continued, a sense of urgency entering her voice, 'I have something to tell you that may come as a shock, but I hope you will accept what I have to say without any judgement.' Charles looked at her, a puzzled expression concealing any sad feelings of a moment ago. 'I think we'd better have another drink' Anne added, hastily pouring a large cognac for Charles and another sherry for herself.

Charles listened, absorbed and totally mesmerized as Anne re-lived her early years. How she had met Sam and their secret liaisons followed ultimately by the birth of Rebecca. He found it difficult to equate Rebecca as Anne's daughter which was not surprising after all this time and he could see and understand how difficult it was for Anne to explain everything now.

'Does Rebecca know any of what you have told me?' 'No' Anne replied adamantly. 'I cannot see the point why she should after all these years. But I'm worried Charles, really worried.' Charles returned her frank gaze. 'What is it Anne? I'm sure you wouldn't have told me such a personal and intimate story unless you had really good reason!' Anne nodded. 'If anything should happen to me Charles, then naturally everything including the land, house, shares, everything will go to Rebecca. But I have heard rumours that her Father, or the person she perceives as her Father, is destitute. He has gambling debts and is well known in London for his high living. I'm sure that if anything happened to me he would worm his way back into Rebecca's life and her possessions.'

Charles' brows knotted together in deep concentration. 'He never cared about Rebecca.' Anne continued, 'He walked out on Sarah when Rebecca was a young child. Since then no-one has heard a word except for an occasional Christmas card.' 'Has he made contact with Rebecca recently?' Charles asked. 'Not that I am aware of' Anne replied. 'Don't worry my dear' Charles added reassuringly, 'I am sure it will never come to anything. But let's get the facts sorted out one by one and then we can put your mind at rest. Anne nodded.

'Thank you Charles. I know I can count on you.' She hesitated before adding, 'Why don't you join me in a light supper.'

Rebecca was somewhat surprised to see the lights still burning in her Aunt's sitting room later that evening on her arrival home. Normally her Aunt was comfortably ensconced in her bed by 10:30 p.m. unless she was enjoying a late game of bridge.

Her Aunt's rooms were located at the front of the rambling mansion with its acres of fertile lush green land. Even following the death of her Mother, her Aunt had continued to occupy the rooms she had grown used to over the years. Self-contained with its oak panelled dining room, separate sitting room, reception area, large kitchen and bedroom with en-suite bathroom, Anne was more than comfortable with her surroundings. Rebecca had respected her Aunt's wish at not moving into the rooms of her now deceased Mother and had gradually accustomed herself to living in the main quarters of the house on her own. Not that she was, in fact, alone. Molly their cook and help and husband Arthur who tended the greenhouse, gardens and odd jobs, were always nearby in their small cottage adjacent to the big house. Two German Shepherds proved worthy watch dogs and were happy roaming the grounds plus one cat, an offspring of her previous cat's dalliance in the village, together with her beautiful mare Ruby, completed the small menagerie. But by Rebecca's standards it was sufficient, especially as she chose to undertake the grooming of Ruby herself.

Rebecca gently tapped on her Aunt's door. 'Come in' came the soft reply. Charles stood in acknowledgement, his arm outstretched in greeting. For a brief moment, Rebecca sensed a certain curiosity in his bright blue eyes which she quickly dismissed to over indulgence in the port and Stilton. Rebecca smiled warmly. 'Charles and I enjoyed a light supper and have been chatting away about old times.' 'Please don't let me disturb you' Rebecca interrupted. 'You're not disturbing us Rebecca' Charles beamed, 'Not at all!' Rebecca wearily settled her long, slim body into the large brown leather armchair, a favourite of hers since as far back as she could remember. 'I saw Gerald this evening' she commented lightly. 'There were eight of us at Fiona Hapsworths' for a cold buffet dinner. Gerald mentioned how busy you all are.' 'That is an understatement my dear' Charles Matthews sighed. 'Did you have a pleasant evening?' Anne asked. 'Yes, it was lovely but I must admit to feeling awfully tired now! You won't mind if I leave you both will you?' 'Of course not' Anne reassured her. 'It was nice of you to pop in. Goodnight my dear.' 'What a delightful young lady she is' Charles commented once Rebecca had left the room.

Chapter 4

THE WARM HIGHLY scented bath water gently soothed Rebecca's tired limbs. It had been a long day and tomorrow she planned an early start in her antique and gift shop in the centre of Roynick. Business had been very good the last few weeks. American tourists were in abundance and over indulgent with their spending, if they managed to find that perfect gift.

Rebecca was looking forward to her next outing to London. There she would attend two of the auction houses. London was always an exciting place to visit. Sometimes she would indulge herself and stay a night or two at the Carlton Tower in Sloane Street, thus enabling her to browse and shop at Harvey Nichols and Harrods nearby. It was always so busy and as much as she loved the hustle and bustle she had to admit that she was a country girl at heart. Once back home she would sigh a long sigh of contentment, happy to be away from all the crowds.

Rebecca's thoughts turned to Gerald Matthews. He was obviously smitten with her and she quite liked him but only in a platonic sort of way. She went out with him occasionally and gathered he hadn't mentioned anything to his Father. Not that it was necessary. He was just one of many admirers in her life at the present time and she certainly did not feel strongly about any of them. Her thoughts wandered back to her meeting that morning. She had been exercising Ruby in the wide open fields when she had abruptly pulled her to a halt. Lying on his back stretched out in the long grass oblivious to all around was a young freckle faced man. He must have been about the same age or a little older than herself. 'My God!' she had exclaimed. 'We could have injured you. Don't you realise that you are completely out of view lying there?' Well, I'm still in one piece' he had replied nonchalantly, 'so no damage done!' Rebecca eyed him curiously. He was extremely attractive in a boyish sort of way. 'Are you from the village?' she asked tentatively, not wishing to appear too inquisitive. 'That I am' he answered, his brown eyes laughing impishly. 'You're from the big house on the hill aren't you?' Rebecca was taken by surprise. Slowly dismounting Ruby, she hesitated before sitting down opposite him in the long grass. 'I'm Mark' he had introduced himself. They had chatted for a while and before leaving Rebecca had made a point of saying that she would look out for him the following week-end, thus avoiding any accidents. Mark had grinned as she mounted Ruby and trotted off.

Rebecca towelled herself dry before cosseting her skin with silky moisturising cream. She was tired and bed beckoned invitingly.

'Tomorrow is another day' she murmured, before slowly drifting off into the realms of another world.

Chapter 5

ROBERT LAWSON AWOKE to a horrendous hangover. His mouth felt like sandpaper and his face bore the marks of excessive over-indulgence. He groaned as he stumbled to the bathroom of his spacious bachelor flat in the centre of London's busy West End. He had been lucky with the flat. He had purchased the 90 year lease the moment he had absconded with part of Sarah's money which he had slowly secreted away during their short lived marriage. An obituary in The Times had brought him the news of her unexpected death nearly two years past and he had subsequently written a letter of condolence to his daughter mindful of the fact that he had not seen her since she was a small child. 'It was not my wish not to see you' he had written, 'but that of your Mother. I hope and pray that with her demise you will, in due course, take it upon yourself to let me visit you and make up a little for the time lost between us. Naturally I respect that a certain period must pass to enable you to come to terms with your grief. Please remember I am here for you, should you wish.

Your Father Robert.'

Nearly two years had elapsed since he had written the letter. Years in which he had slowly but surely squandered the remaining wealth from his third society marriage. On reflection life with Sarah hadn't been that bad. She had not been demanding like his last two wives but life in the country after returning from the war earlier than most due to a leg injury, had proved too boring and complacent for him to say the least.

He admitted he had never been head over heels in love with Sarah. Marriage into the Henderson estate was a coup d'etat and life as a gentleman squire was much to be relished. The birth of his daughter was another bonus and returning to Roynick he was able to spend the first couple of years doting on his child. He remembered how she would cry and her round little cheeks would puff out in temper when he picked her up and cuddled her in his arms. Yes, he admitted to himself, he loved her, doted on her in the beginning, until the novelty began to wear . 'If you cry I'm having nothing to do with you' he would scold. Then in a selfish temper he would thrust her into the arms of her loving Mother and stalk off to his private sitting room. Gradually he began to accept the fact that as soon as his stock broking took off, so would he. It was then he devised a plan to rid Sarah of some of her wealth. He didn't feel guilty about it. 'Why should I?' he would mutter to himself. 'Without me she would not have Rebecca and the respect that comes with our family name.' Unbeknown to him, Sarah couldn't have cared less about family titles and secretly made jokes about her husband's snobbishness. 'Don't be such a bore.' she would tease, 'No-one cares tuppence who your family were!' 'What would you know about that' he would reply sardonically. 'Your parents inherited land, not nobility!' and he would stalk out of the room again adding, 'that can never be bred into you my dear!' Sarah would sigh in disbelief. But she trusted Robert as a stockbroker with her money and his knowledge of the banking world. But the stock market was very depressed and never for one moment did she suspect that he could have been pocketing her money on the side. It was only when he at least had the courtesy to say he was leaving, that the idea flashed as a warning signal across her mind. Unfortunately, by then, it was too late and she chastised herself at having been so foolishly naïve in trusting him so implicitly despite his grotesque and uncaring ways. 'Good riddance and all that' her sister Anne would always say when she was in one of her woeful states. 'Just thank the Lord you have Rebecca' deep down thankful herself that the good Lord had instigated the departure of such an awful man from their midst.

Robert Lawson grimaced as the icy water made contact with the tired puffy skin around his eyes. He knew some worthwhile tricks and this was one of them. It was a miracle, this metamorphosis that unfolded slowly but surely before him. A brusque shower, hot then cold, followed by a wet shave, (no stupid electrical appliance for him), then a good rub down followed by a liberal sprinkling of after shave and body lotion, and lo and behold, he was, once more the debonair man about town again. He fleetingly wondered about calling Lady Cynthia Cope to join him for dinner. She was good to be seen with and as his senior by a few years, over indulgent with her money. 'Cynthia, I must cash a cheque' he would gently murmur in her ear.' 'Don't be silly Robert' she would chide. 'I've plenty of cash with me. There's no need for that.' Robert would make sure that she would enjoy a first class meal with her customary bottle of Dom Perignon and Beluga caviar but fortunately it did not cost him one penny. The Clarice Club knew and respected Mr. Robert Lawson. Over the years he had lost and won, the former being more obvious, and he also had a talent for introducing the wealthiest of clients to the private club. His wining and dining at the Clarice was for them an exercise in public relations and his losing, an added bonus. His patronage at the club was welcomed with open arms. His thoughts slowly turned to Rebecca. It was time he made contact with her once more. Surely his daughter had grieved sufficiently to come to terms with her Mother's death. He felt he really wanted to see her, to admire his only offspring after such a long absence. It was his right! He was her Father no matter what. That was something she would never be able to deny. But how could he ever convince Rebecca that Sarah was the one who stopped him from spending time with her as she grew up. Well he thought. One step at a time!

Chapter 6

REBECCA FOUND HERSELF looking forward to her week-end meetings with Mark. Fortunately the weather had been kind and she was able to sit and chat to him in the privacy of the expanse of grass which blanketed the fields around. Under her guidance and instruction, Mark was also finding his confidence in riding her mare. She laughed at his obvious inexperience but in time came to respect his steadfast perseverance.

'I can't believe how well you ride now' she would exclaim, 'and in such a short time'. A huge grin would cover Mark's face from ear to ear and his light brown hair would emphasise the freckles spattered across his face. Mark adored Rebecca but would not, he told himself, become involved in any way. He was just the lad from the village and she was from the House on the Hill. Yes, they enjoyed one another's company for a chat and now a ride but that was where it stopped. Rebecca had suggested they might enjoy a snack in town but Mark had thought otherwise. 'She's different' he confided in his Mother. 'I know you would think so too.' His Mother hardly paid any attention to his words. Mark understood. There had been many stories about the folks on the hill, how wealthy they were but not unkind too. But somehow the village people kept themselves apart. They watched them on Sundays dressed up in their riding habits, quaffing their pints of beer and gin and tonics. But what they disliked was the sound of the dogs barking excitedly on their way to the hunt and those poor foxes being chased this way and that. Rebecca's friends had given up in their quest for her to join the hunt. She had told them in her straight forward and direct honest manner that she had no intention of hunting any poor defenceless wild creatures but if they found it in their hearts to do so, then sobeit! Mark shuddered. 'Rebecca doesn't hunt Mother. She doesn't believe that it's right or Godly to do so.' His Mother just nodded.

'Why is your Mother so against us?' Rebecca asked, her head resting lightly on Mark's knee. It was a beautiful day, hardly a cloud in the sky with only a faint breeze lingering around them. 'It's because they think you don't have to work for your money and life's easy for all you and your kind.' 'That's unfair' Rebecca retorted angrily. 'I work hard in my shop and my grandparents worked the land themselves until they could afford to buy it. No-one thinks about that.' Mark looked at her somewhat apologetically. 'They aren't my thoughts' he added defensively. 'You asked me about my Mother and other folks. If you don't want a true answer you shouldn't ask.' 'I'm sorry' Rebecca apologised.

They both sat for a while before tucking into the picnic basket which Molly had prepared earlier that morning. 'I was told your Father was a Lord or something' Mark commented hesitantly. Rebecca's cheeks flushed. 'I haven't seen my Father for years' she paused. 'He did write when he heard of my Mother's death and said I should contact him if I wanted.' 'And do you want to?' Mark asked. 'I don't know' Rebecca replied vaguely. 'I really don't know'. Mark watched her sensing that she was brooding inside and kicked himself for mentioning her Father. Why did he always have the habit of putting his foot in it. 'I'm still starving' he pleaded, desperate to change the subject. 'Is there any more where that came from?'

Chapter 7

THE FOLLOWING MORNING brought a bundle of mail, mostly business. A carefully handwritten envelope with its London postmark jolted Rebecca's thoughts. It had been nearly two years since she had last received a similar envelope and even the intervening Christmas period had not brought forth the customary greetings card.

Rebecca had read in all the gossip columns, which she followed avidly, the news that her Father had divorced yet again and that he was often to be seen at the exclusive gambling clubs in London. Typical, Rebecca had thought each time his picture appeared. Her Mother had made her aware on the rare occasions when she mentioned her Father, of his inbred snobbishness.

Rebecca's fingers trembled slightly as she opened the carefully sealed envelope.

'My Dear Rebecca' it began.

'I now feel that sufficient time has elapsed since the passing of your Mother for us to finally meet again. I would like you to come to London and possibly stay with a dear friend of mine, Lady Cynthia Cope. We could spend ample time together and when, or if this becomes difficult, Lady Cope would be a delightful companion and would be really happy to show you her collection of antiques which we both are sure you would enjoy immensely. I am of course sure there are many questions you would like to ask me and I would appreciate the opportunity to answer them with all frankness and sincerity. My time is yours, if you wish! That is all I can ask of you. Meanwhile please give my request a little thought and whatever you decide, please remember I am always here for you!

Your Father Robert'

P.S I would invite you to stay at my apartment but I think you would be more comfortable in the spacious rooms of Lady Cope's residence in Cadogan Square.'

Rebecca read the letter a second time before placing it in the drawer of her writing bureau. She would have a chance to discuss it later with Aunt Anne over dinner. She felt so terribly confused. Deep down she did want to see her Father but inside she felt a deep hurt and resentment for all the years without him. It was a known fact that her Mother had never wished her to meet him but there were so many unanswered questions that only he would ever be able to explain.

Rebecca heaved a troubled sigh before descending the stairs and bade farewell to Molly who was busy polishing a large canteen of silver cutlery. 'I'll be joining Aunt Anne this evening for dinner' she added, before leaving the house and driving off in her light blue mini.

Dinner consisted of consommé followed by poached salmon, new potatoes and baby peas together with a lightly tossed salad. Dessert comprised of fresh fruit laced with brandy. Molly prided herself on her culinary offerings and saw to it that the two ladies in her charge were kept on a healthy diet. 'You won't be needing all those vitamin pills they keep advertising if you eat my fayre' was one of her favourite sayings. 'No need to be wasting your money on all of that!'

Anne watched Rebecca toying with her food. She knew these were signs of nervousness and wondered what Rebecca was about to tell her. All in good time, she thought, not wishing to press the issue. She knew Rebecca so well. Many of her mannerisms reminded her of when she was young but fortunately Rebecca didn't have to contend with a domineering elder sister and had acquired far more confidence in her own self-worth. In some ways Anne had often thought that a brother or sister would have provided a friend and confidante for Rebecca, but on the other hand, one could never tell. There again any offspring from Robert Lawson! She shuddered dismissing the thought immediately.

'I received a letter from Father this morning.' Rebecca hesitated. 'He asked if I would like to join him in London for a couple of days.' Rebecca handed the letter to her Aunt. Anne read the letter, a look of disbelief clouding her eyes. 'Well' she commented, trying hard to hide the feelings of contempt from her voice, 'how do you feel about seeing him?' 'I don't know' Rebecca stammered. 'It's difficult. I know what he says about Mother is true. She never wanted us to meet. On the other hand perhaps there is more to it than Mother ever told me. Perhaps it wasn't solely his fault that he never saw me!' Anne frowned, 'Rebecca your Mother was always honest with you.' The words stuck in her throat as she realised their very meaning. Never in her wildest imagination did she dream that events would begin to catch up with the past in such an unexpected way. 'Are you all right?' Rebecca asked, concerned at her Aunt's obvious momentary distress. 'Yes, yes. It's just that I find it hard to accept that your Father after all these years can now suddenly want to wear the mantle of a parent. I find it really ironic.' 'I understand your feelings' Rebecca interrupted, 'I really do but please try to understand mine!' 'I do!' Anne responded. 'All I ask is that whatever you decide and whatever happens you will always be totally honest with me.' 'I will. I promise!' Rebecca reassured her, placing a light kiss on her Aunt's worried brow.

Chapter 8

ANNE HARDLY SLEPT that night as she tossed and turned in her bed. It seemed as though she was suddenly being confronted with her worst fears. 'It didn't take him long.' she thought wryly. 'Just sufficient time for Rebecca to have come to terms with her grief and in he steps.' She longed to ring Charles Matthews but considered it too late. Their relationship since their first dinner had been kindled over the past weeks. Fortunately he was now aware of all the facts concerning Rebecca so she could unload, selfishly perhaps, a little of her worries and fears onto his broad shoulders. He was such a practical man. Mrs. Matthews had been fortunate in her choice of husband. Her thoughts wandered back in time to Sam. Two small gentle tears trickled down her pale cheeks. 'What can I do Sam?' she begged. 'Please guide me now. We mustn't hurt our daughter Sam. We mustn't hurt her. Too much is at stake.' Anne could see Sarah's pallid face mirrored before her. The pain Sarah experienced throughout her unexpected illness must have been insufferable. But Sarah had always been strong. God had prepared her in his own way. No one ever saw the real extent to which she had had suffered. 'There's nothing we can do now that the cancer has spread' the Harley Street Specialist was finally forced to admit. 'Only pray' Anne had added quietly, 'only pray. Sarah, why did you have to leave us?' Anne sobbed, 'Sarah, please understand that what I did was for you as well as Rebecca' but deep down Anne was beginning to wonder whether she had been selfish and uncaring with her reasoning. Yes she had only been a young girl at the time and now she was beginning to doubt and chastise herself and her motives. 'I only did what I thought was best' she mumbled before finally falling into a fitful sleep.

Chapter 9

CHARLES MATTHEWS MADE a mental note of the time before greeting his 11:00 client. He had told Anne he would endeavour to be with her by 3p.m but with a luncheon meeting scheduled for 1p.m (if everything progressed according to plan) he knew he was cutting it rather fine. 'Don't worry my dear' he had reassured her earlier that morning at the sound of panic in her voice, 'I'll be with you as early as I can.' 'You do realise' she had whispered falteringly, 'that I really don't wish to go into any details over the phone!' 'Yes my dear. I do.' He had replaced the receiver in deep thought. It was unusual for Anne to be alarmed at anything and he wondered whether her fears had been realised regarding their discussion some weeks back. 'Not possible' he muttered to himself, 'I doubt that it will ever come to that!'

Anne had awoken with a migraine. It pressed heavily over her right eye and throbbed unrelentingly in her temple. She knew that once it took hold with its vice like grip, it could completely take over for at least a couple of days. From her bathroom cabinet she found one of the specially prescribed tablets and waited anxiously as it slowly dissolved, gently bubbling in its bed of water. Having forced some cereal into her empty stomach, she swallowed the noxious mixture, praying it would come to the rescue soon. She toyed with the idea of taking half a sedative to help it on its way, then dismissing the thought returned to her bed for another hour's sleep feeling a little more settled with the knowledge of Charles' impending visit. Thank goodness he was aware of all the facts. It seemed as if everything she had imagined was now falling into place. 'Could this be the beginning of a nightmare?' she asked herself. 'Were all her recent fears now to be realised?'

Rebecca had left the house very early that morning. 'I won't disturb you before I leave' she had told her Aunt the previous evening. Fortunately for Anne, Rebecca had, as usual, kept her word thereby not witnessing the tired lines which now bore their marks across her Aunt's face.

Drawing the heavy brocade curtains tightly together blotting out the bright sunshine, Anne soon fell into a comfortable sleep only to be awoken by a light tapping on her bedroom door. 'Will you be wanting lunch?' Molly's soft voice asked. 'I'm sorry Molly' Anne replied apologetically. 'I omitted to mention to you that I didn't feel too well this morning. Yes, that will be fine but only something very light. Perhaps some scrambled eggs on toast would be a good idea!'

The warm bath water felt good as Anne tried to relax her tense muscles. A dull ache persisted over her right eye and temple but she was thankful it hadn't progressed. She had selected a comfortable light woollen trouser suit with a silk cream blouse and flat beige shoes. The colour was peaceful, a mood she needed reflected around her during this worrying time. She wondered what Charles would advise her to do but there was no point thinking about it until their meeting.

At 3:15 p.m the sound of Charles' car on the gravel outside the house brought a great sense of relief. A pot of Earl Grey tea and plate of assorted biscuits awaited his arrival in her small sitting room.

'How are you feeling now my dear?' he enquired on entering the room. Molly quietly closed the door behind them, curious at this unusual time of visit. 'The worst has happened Charles' Anne stammered, trying to curb the emotion which tempered her voice. 'Rebecca told me last night she had received a letter from her Father. He wishes her to consider visiting him Charles, and needless to say, I am very worried.' 'Now, now my dear' Charles tried to pacify her, 'you're still here, alive and well and there's nothing he can do at the present time.' 'But I am worried Charles, very worried. Rebecca has her own income plus her trust fund which pays out on a regular basis. Granted she doesn't have access to the estate, land and shares but what if he begins to worm his way into her life now. What will happen later?' 'Honestly Anne, I think you are worrying unnecessarily. But forewarned is forearmed and it is better we look at the situation as it now stands.' Charles paused for a moment, taking advantage of the opportunity to reflect on the situation whilst drinking his tea. 'Did Rebecca tell you what she plans to do?' he asked quietly, not wishing to add further to Anne's obvious distress. 'No, not exactly. She really wasn't sure but I know her overriding curiosity will get the better of her eventually. Charles what should I do? I've already told her that her Mother' she hesitated for a moment, 'that Sarah was right in what she said and did. I can't convince her that her Father' she paused again, a slight tinge of colour stabbing her cheeks, 'did have access to her but couldn't be bothered and had no interest to visit her. I'm in a very difficult situation Charles, you know that'. 'Yes Anne, I do, but I feel everything has happened far too quickly and perhaps you are not being objective enough about the situation.' Anne looked at Charles, slightly puzzled by his last remark. 'Please Anne, trust me!' Charles continued. 'I think you must let Rebecca make her own decisions and I'm sure you will find in time that you've caused yourself unnecessary worry.' 'I hope so Charles' Anne added despondently, 'I only hope you're right!'

Chapter 10

'YOU'RE LOOKING TIRED' Rebecca commented sympathetically on greeting her Aunt for dinner. 'It's just one of my migraines' Anne replied lightly, disguising the turmoil she was feeling inside. 'Are you playing bridge on Friday?' Rebecca asked. 'Yes my dear, but not here. Jean and Arthur have made up two rubbers at their place and we'll have a light supper beforehand.' 'I'm thinking of having a few friends over for a dinner party that evening' Rebecca added. 'Fiona said she would love to come and I know Gerald is free. Miles Rose is here for two weeks from London and Sarah Worthington has been dying to meet him.' 'That means you're one male short' Anne calculated. 'Yes, I know but I'm sure Roger will come. He's such fun although a little pompous at times. I expect I'd better make some calls as this isn't much notice'.

Rebecca gently fondled her Aunt's hand before hurrying away to her room. She had experienced a rather hectic and unsettling day. Although her Aunt had tried to conceal her disapproval Rebecca knew that she wasn't happy at the thought of a possible reconciliation with her Father. But as much as she appreciated her Aunt's feelings, she felt very strongly that this was a matter which was her responsibility alone and even though she loved and respected her Aunt, she had to make her own decisions. It was difficult, given the circumstances, but it was something she had to do, irrespective of what the outcome would be.

Lifting up the telephone she called her friends and as an afterthought made two more calls, bringing the total number for Friday evening to eight. With the dinner party plans finalised, she opened the drawer of her writing bureau and retrieved her Father's letter which she read and re-read before slowly and thoughtfully settling down to reply.

By Friday evening, Anne was feeling much more relaxed. Rebecca had not mentioned the letter, or unbeknown to Anne the reply which now rested in the drawer of her writing bureau awaiting postage.

Anne bade farewell to Rebecca and Molly before leaving for her bridge evening at the Jacksons. 'I have no idea what time I'll be home' she told Molly before climbing into her Bentley. 'Possibly not until one o'clock knowing us'. Molly grinned, happy to see Miss Henderson in better spirits. It had puzzled her considerably to see her mistress so low and at one point she had expected her to come down with some sort of flu bug. But then, Molly had reasoned, that didn't necessarily tie in with the unusual afternoon visit of Mr. Matthews. 'There's something funny going on!' she told her husband 'Something very strange to be sure!' 'What nonsense are your talking' Arthur had retorted. 'You've too much of an imagination woman, that's your problem. Not enough work to keep you busy is more what I'd say!' 'Oh do be shutting your mouth' Molly replied curtly. 'Women are much more intuitive than men. Mark my words, we're going to be hearing more in time. You mark my words!'

The dinner party was a total success. Miles as always was good company and away from the Merchant Bankers in the city, he loved to unwind back in his hometown of Roynick. A handsome, dark, slim young man, he was still enjoying his bachelor status and as such was always eager to meet a pretty young new face on the scene, even if he did have the tendency to love them and leave them. Rebecca had known him from as far back as she could remember and made a point of warning Sarah of his reputation. 'Fast cars, fast girls and fast living' she had joked. 'Just be on your guard!' Sarah had smiled, not worrying about, as she put it, those minor details. 'Well you can't say I haven't warned you' Rebecca added seriously, not wishing to have the problem of another love sick damsel in distress crying on her shoulder. She despaired at the thought of having to help pick up all the pieces once again! Roger was full of his awful jokes which despite their mediocrity made them all laugh helped along by bottles of red and white wine. Gerald as always, attended on Rebecca and during the course of the evening she found her thoughts straying to Mark. By midnight they were settled in the comfortable lounge watching the latest released video which Miles had brought with him. Anne could hear their laughter as she entered the house and quietly made her way to her room not wishing to intrude.

Chapter 11

MARK WAS CONTENTEDLY sunning himself lying in the long tall grass. The familiar sound of Rebecca and Ruby cantering across the fields brought a smile to his tanned face. It was good to be here, he thought. Good to be away from his busy car repair workshop. He had worked hard to get that far. Even as far as studying at night school to pass his exams. And his parents had been right. 'You've got to be able to stand on your own two feet in this world' his Mother would always say. 'Look at your Dad. Always cap in hand to someone else. That's not for you son. Not for you.' And she was right. He had worked all hours of the day and night to build up his reputation and to meet the increasing demands of his customers. But now it had paid off and he was never short of work. He'd even seen some of his competition fold up but there was nothing he could do about that, but he did make a point of referring smaller jobs, which he had no time to handle, to Percy Baker on the other side of the village. They had both been at school together and Mark was consistently loyal to his friends. 'Never a beggar or borrower be' his Father would always say. 'God gave you a healthy body and a good pair of hands son. Use them as he intended.' And he had.

'Gosh, you were deep in thought' Rebecca laughed as she dismounted Ruby. 'Just thinking' Mark retorted in his shy, masculine way. 'Sometimes when I lie here with only the sky, the sun and the gentle breeze around me, I find myself thinking about so many things. Things I would never normally think about. But then I say to myself, you're going soft in the head Mark Black, you're going soft in the head!' Rebecca laughed. He looked so serious. 'I know what you mean. I really do. But what I find good for me is riding Ruby and when we're galloping or cantering through the fields with the wind rushing past my face and through my hair, I think of nothing. It's incredible. My mind becomes totally free!'

Mark rolled over onto his side and began fumbling with a brown paper bag.. 'I've made us some sandwiches and I've also included a couple of Ma's homemade Cornish pasties.' 'Mmm, that sounds good,' Rebecca commented settling down on the rug beside him. 'What have you brought to drink?' 'You'd thought I'd forgotten' he reprimanded her jokingly. 'Ice tea with lemon My Lady'. 'Perfect' Rebecca smiled, 'who could ask for anything more.'

The day passed peacefully with no-one to disturb them. Mark took Ruby for a gallop and flushed with the exercise settled down beside Rebecca once more. Deep down something was troubling him. Prior to his first encounter with Rebecca he had been practically engaged to a young girl from the village. But now she held no excitement for him and he found their time together becoming less and less. He had not told Rebecca about her. He hadn't thought it necessary. His Mother had noticed though and made wry little comments. 'Is Wendy all right son? You haven't brought her home for a few weeks now.' Mark shrugged his shoulders. He really had no desire to discuss Wendy or anything else. He had tried to explain a little about Rebecca but his Mother was ruthlessly indifferent to his words. 'Stay with your own kind son. I've seen this all before and it never works.' 'I don't intend asking her to marry me Ma. She's only a friend' his Mother tutted. 'There's no such thing as a friend of the female sex' she scoffed. 'Just stay with your own, it's for your own good.'

'Mark' Rebecca's voice startled him back to the present. 'Mark, I received a letter from my Father a few days ago.' 'You what?' he exclaimed. 'I thought you told me that he never kept in touch with you?' 'Yes, that's true' Rebecca nodded. 'He wrote to me when he heard of my Mother's death and since then I haven't heard a word until now.' 'What does he want?' Mark asked curiously, 'Nothing really only to see me.' 'Why didn't he see you before?' Mark commented, feeling he had put his foot right in it once more. 'He says Mother would never allow him to see me and I know that there is some truth in that.' 'I suppose she had her reasons' Mark added seriously. 'Perhaps she never told you everything in case it would hurt your feelings.' 'I don't know' Rebecca hesitated, nervously toying with a few strands of grass. 'I don't know but I do think it is time I found out.'

'Where does he want to see you?' Mark asked inquisitively. 'He asked if I would stay at a lady friend's home in London. He thinks it would be less of a strain in case we don't get on too well.' 'So when are you going?' 'Once I post my reply, probably the weekend after next. I wanted to ask your advice before posting it. Mark stared at Rebecca in surprise. 'My advice?' he questioned. 'How can you ask me for advice?' 'Like this' Rebecca responded, gently placing his face in her hands and kissing each and every freckle she could see. 'Like this Mark. It's really very, very easy!'

Chapter 12

THE SOUND OF the early morning post being pushed violently through the letterbox disturbed Robert Lawson's slumbering hangover. As usual, after a full night's non-stop, binging he felt disastrous. Lying completely naked in his bed, the duvet half straggled on the floor, he gazed up at the bare white ceiling pondering his fate.

'Is this what my life amounts to?' he asked self pityingly. 'Is this all I have strived for over all these years?' Turning over onto his side he fiddled with the knob of the cream bakelite antique radio, a relic that had survived his many years and his one and only attachment to the past.

His thoughts slowly turned to Cynthia. She hadn't been with him last evening, 'and that's why I'm in such a bloody awful mess now!' he exclaimed out loud. This sudden violent reaction disturbed him. 'For Christ's sake' he groaned, 'what could I have been thinking?' But finally he had no option but to admit it. Amazingly uncharacteristic as it might seem, he really did enjoy being with Lady Cynthia Cope and it wasn't due solely to her generous nature with her vast amount of wealth. Somehow Robert Lawson found himself totally shocked by these unexpected thoughts. 'Jesus Christie, the woman's no bimbo. She's at least nine years my senior and that's ludicrous'. But ludicrous or not he had to admit that for once nature was having the last laugh. 'Lady Cynthia Cope' he murmured, 'a widow with over adequate fortunes. No-one in heaven's name would ever think it remotely possible. No-one not even Cynthia herself'. He was absolutely right of course. No-one would. His reputation as a philandering fortune hunter had preceded him and he was well aware that Lady Cynthia was no fool no matter what feminine guile she strew in his path.

Faces of his previous brides and mistresses drifted across his mind. His last two wives had been society beauties and young enough to be his daughters. Jennifer had been the epitome of over indulgence and empty headedness. 'Why did I marry her?' he wondered. But he didn't wonder for too long. Fortunately for Jennifer, her Father still played a dominant role in her shallow life and he made sure she was not stripped of her fortunes by this philandering chancer. He had warned her, of course. It didn't take an ounce of brain to suss out Robert Lawson. Admittedly his background was good. Public school educated and a titled family, but what else was there in his favour? Nothing! But Jennifer, spoilt, over bearing child that she was wouldn't hear a word of it. 'Daddy, you're so cwuel' she would whimper with her aggravating lisp. 'I do believe you are jealous.' Robert could still hear her high pitched shrill voice now. 'Ugh' he shuddered, trying desperately to blot out the sound. 'Ugh!' Their marriage had survived two long tedious years. But Robert Lawson had to pay the price for his shallow existence and two years was a sentence which seemed like eternity.

He pummelled his pillow trying desperately to blot out any further visions, but too late. Camilla Lloyd-Payne's gamine looks peered back at him. 'What the hell' he muttered out loud. Ten years of marriage to that bitch should have cured him for life. Thank God he hadn't loved her. That conniving whore! Oh yes, he admitted to himself, he'd had the rambling estate which Daddy had provided and her horses and groom. They had had the last laugh. It had all been much too convenient. Much too convenient indeed but he Robert Lawson was to self- smitten to notice. They had known of his distasteful ways, of his fawning over available assets. No-one had uttered one word of disapproval. Not one! Admitted Camilla had suffered a miscarriage but that was a bloody lucky escape. He had felt genuinely sorry for her at the time but, deep down, thankful nevertheless. But the thunderbolt really hurt his pride and masculinity arriving home unexpectedly to find her in bed with the groom, nakedly entwined in one another's arms oblivious to his stunned image, standing half hidden behind the partially closed door listening to their panting and squeals of delight and ecstasy. That was bad enough. But another woman was more than he had ever bargained for! Two large bulbous breasts pressing down like heavy balloons on two smaller firmer mounds. He could see them now. How ridiculous they looked, their two bodies writhing, hands between each other's legs where normally his fully extended penis probed. His wife, Camilla Lloyd-Payne a lesbian! That was more than he could ever take and how everyone must have laughed. Split their sides from laughing. He Robert Lawson in his search for easily accessible wealth had been too caught up in his own devious deeds not to have noticed. 'How could they have used me?' he had demanded of a close friend. 'They bloody well knew she was a lesbian. How humiliating! How could they!' Yes, they had used him. He had provided the adequate cover for their precious daughter until by the slightest of flukes he had discovered the truth.

'Why did he have to come home so unexpectedly?' Camilla wailed. Everything had been working so perfectly well. They were invited to all the elitist parties and the scandal making, muck raking gossips had been thwarted in their tracks. Her escapades in the past had been put down to adolescence and she was free of their sneering looks and caustic remarks.

'Why did that lousy bastard have to spoil it all?' She sobbed once more entwined in the fleshy cavernous arms of her lover. She had even suggested to Robert that they continue their marriage in name only following in the footsteps of their many titled friends. Even suggested a ménage a trois as an enticement, playing on his more basic and perverted instincts but surprisingly enough,

Robert found these circumstances too much for him to accept and took solace in the fact that perhaps there was a spark of decency left in him after all, somewhere!

His thoughts disjointedly turned to Sarah. 'Ah well' he sighed, 'that was different. I was too young, too ambitious and unsettled by the war. Many young men had found themselves in a similar situation caught up in the traumatic emotions of the time. Making hasty decisions they would have time enough to regret later. Deep down he was genuinely sorry for the hurt he had caused, but it was too late now, except of course for Rebecca, the daughter who had grown so rapidly into a mature young woman. The daughter he had selfishly neglected and missed. But in time, he vowed to himself he would do the right thing by her. In time!

The persistent ringing of the telephone forced Robert Lawson to temporarily postpone the rituals of his morning ablutions. 'Cynthia' he gushed, 'how nice of you to call.' 'For heaven's sake Robert' Cynthia's voice rasped, 'Don't give me all that bullshit!' Robert, momentarily taken aback, remained silent. 'Are you still among the living?' Cynthia asked, a hint of sarcasm creeping into her voice. 'I'm sorry my dear' Robert apologised. 'And so you should be!' Cynthia interrupted. 'I heard you overdid it again last night. Must I be around to keep you on the straight and narrow all the time?' Robert smiled. 'Yes my dear. Now what can I do for you?' 'Nothing' Cynthia replied, 'It's what can I do for you!' 'Well what can you do Cynthia, taking into consideration that I am standing here dripping wet from top to toe having rushed out of the shower to answer your call!' 'You really are wet!' Cynthia laughed enjoying the pun. 'Well don't stand there like a fish out of water' she laughed again 'can you join me at my place for lunch?' ' Is there any reason?' Robert questioned. 'No nothing that you won't be able to handle. 1:00 p.m. ok?' And with a deep chuckle she replaced the receiver.

Robert returned to the bathroom making a mental note of the time. He had a couple of matters to attend to for a client, that didn't entail travelling to the city, so there was no need to rush.

Having completed his routine and coddled in his navy and red towelling robe, he collected his mail and newspapers from the door mat cursing at the batch of bills which greeted him. The feminine writing on the discreetly perfumed envelope came as an unexpected surprise. Hurriedly placing the newspapers and remaining envelopes on the breakfast table he carefully opened the neat envelope.

'Dear Father,

I do hope you are well. I admit I was rather surprised to receive your letter after such a long while. Yes, I do miss Mother very, very much but I am now coming to terms with her death. Aunt Anne has been a great comfort. I mentioned to her that you had asked to see me. In all honesty she is far from happy at the thought. But I have decided I will meet with you at Lady

Cynthia's but I cannot make any promises as to my reaction at what you may have to say.

I would prefer to arrive on a Friday evening and travel back to Roynick the following Monday. I will call you at home next Wednesday evening at around 9:30 p.m. to confirm the arrangements.

Rebecca'

Robert was surprised to find he was not alone on arriving at Cadogan Square. The sound of animated chatter greeted him as he entered the square airy hallway. Robinson greeted him with his usual perfunctory politeness, at the same time ushering him through to the drawing room. 'Robert my dear' Cynthia enthused at the same time placing a light kiss on his cheek. 'I'm so pleased you could come at such short notice!' Robert returned her greeting with a quick wink. 'Bullshit' he whispered in her ear.

Her arm encircling his Cynthia guided him towards a rather handsome young man deeply engrossed in conversation with a younger man and woman. 'David' Cynthia, gently interrupted, 'I would like to introduce my very dear friend, Robert Lawson.' Robert shook hands curiously wondering what part David played in Cynthia's life. 'David's my son' Cynthia explained, a mischievous twinkle reflecting in her eyes. 'And I would like you to meet Rosemary, my niece, David's daughter and her husband Ashley Montague.' 'Delighted, delighted,' Robert murmured, momentary taken aback by the intimacy of the luncheon party. 'I wanted you to come Robert,' Cynthia whispered, 'it isn't often I have three of the family here at one time and I did so want you to meet them.'

Lunch was a relaxed and enjoyable event. It transpired that Rosemary and her husband spent most of their time in Wiltshire where Ashley had his own estate agency. David, on the other hand, had his own Veterinary Practice in Portland Street and was always at a loss for free time. 'David's very well respected in his field,' Cynthia proudly boasted. 'Unfortunately she continued 'his ex-wife didn't share his total commitment to our four-legged friends, hence the ex!' 'Oh well' Robert responded, 'It happens to the best of us at times. By the way Cynthia, may I have a private word with you before I leave?'

Somewhat apprehensively, Robert produced the perfumed envelope from his jacket pocket and handed it to Cynthia. 'Don't worry' she fondled his hand affectionately; 'I'll make sure that Rebecca is welcomed as I would my own. Rest assured I won't cause you any embarrassment and will respect the need for privacy.'

Robert felt a great weight lifted from his shoulders. He could rely on Cynthia to do the right thing. For once he felt there was someone he wanted the right thing by too. And, Rebecca, of course!

Chapter 13

ANNE KNEW WHAT Rebecca was about to tell her even before she had begun. Although deep down she felt a little hurt that despite her obvious feeling Rebecca has still decided to meet with her Father, she had to admit that in Rebecca's situation she would, in all probability, have reacted in the same way. She had been somewhat surprised to learn that Rebecca would be staying with Lady Cynthia Cope. Anne knew of her and also the fact that she was older than Robert Lawson. Not that the difference in a woman's age bothered her in the slightest but in Robert Lawson it was a complete deviation from the norm. 'He's up to his usual tricks' she thought despairingly. 'Now he's picking on older women instead of the usual nymphets half his age!' 'I thought Friday week would be a good time to visit and I'd drive back the following Monday.' 'Why don't you take the train?' Anne suggested. 'I would' Rebecca replied, 'but it will be easier with the car. I'm not sure exactly how long it will take and I don't feel like lugging a week-end case around with me.' Anne nodded. She had noticed over the weeks a gradual change in Rebecca. What it was she could not pinpoint exactly. Gerald Matthews appeared to be playing a more important role in Rebecca's life but there again, perhaps it was her imagination. Until Rebecca actually told her so, she had no intention of prying.

The remainder of the week seemed to drag as Rebecca anxiously awaited her next meeting with Mark. She was becoming frustrated with their weekend trysts and had decided to tell Mark how this was affecting her. 'It's ridiculous only meeting here at weekends' she had blurted out whilst rummaging through an assortment of sandwiches which she had prepared herself earlier that morning. 'Why can't we meet up in the week, have dinner, see a movie or something?' Mark hesitated for a moment before replying, 'how can we? I'm not one of your kind. You can't be seen with me!' 'That's rubbish!' Rebecca interrupted angrily, 'It's you who is a snob not me nor my friends. Can't you see that?' 'Well!' she continued, haven't you anything to say?' 'Don't be silly' Mark stammered, 'You know it's not me.' 'Who is it then?' she retorted, a defiant expression creeping across her face. 'Why don't you let me come to your home and meet your parents? Why won't you be seen with me in the village? Perhaps you've someone else that I don't know about!' Mark's face coloured. 'I told you I was seeing Wendy but I don't love her' he added falteringly. 'I think I'm in love with you.'

Rebecca's eyes misted over with tears, 'Oh Mark' she sighed, 'you don't know how long I've waited for you to tell me that.' 'Dear Rebecca' Mark repeated, gently gathering her close in his arms.

Chapter 14

LADY CYNTHIA COPE busied herself arranging a vase of mixed summer flowers. She had chosen the prettiest guest room for Rebecca's stay and wanted everything to be absolutely perfect. Normally on such occasions it was the responsibility of her maid to organise such details but as it was Robert's daughter and their meeting was so crucial, she intended to involve herself as much as possible.

Cynthia reflected on how sad it was that Rebecca had grown up not knowing her Father. Robert had explained the difficulties he had experienced with his ex-wife Sarah, Anne's elder sister, and had also mentioned how immature he had behaved during their marriage. 'It was a long time ago Cynthia and with the upheaval of the war some of us reacted by doing stupid things.' Cynthia understood. She remembered those years only too well and the strains imposed on family life. Her husband was hardly ever at home during that time and everyone had to pitch in. Living in the centre of London had been no joke, always a target of the most horrific attacks from the Luftwaffe. It was with great relief when Lord Henry insisted that she and her young daughter Jemma move to the country for a while away from the bombing, the sirens and the catastrophic upheaval. By then she was pregnant with her second child. 'Those bastards will kill you and our children' he had muttered over and over again. And he had nearly been right. It was only by sheer luck their home remained unscathed although the devastation around was nearly too much to bear. Fortunately the birth of their son David was uncomplicated and as with so many families during that time they made the best of whatever they had.

Deep down Cynthia blamed the war for Jemma's strong independent streak. Once she had reached her 20th birthday Jemma announced to her parents that she intended travelling the world by any means available. 'We can't stop her' Cynthia had pleaded with her husband, and he had finally relented. 'She should have been a boy' he would mumble under his breath, deeply inhaling on one of his favourite cigars accompanied by a large brandy. 'She should have been a boy!' But it wasn't long before they received a letter telling of her plans to marry in South Africa. 'He's very nice' Jemma had written, 'and I know you will approve of your new son-in-law to be.' Fortunately they had approved and with the profits her husband Desmond was making out of the diamond business, she was the proud inhabitant of a beautiful house with gardens and swimming pool in an exclusive suburb outside Johannesburg. With the war behind them, Cynthia had found herself worrying about the political aspects of her daughter's new found home. Apartheid, segregation of whites and blacks, was a situation she found utterly deplorable. 'Mother there's nothing at all for you to worry about' Jemma would try to reassure her. 'But there'll be a blood bath there soon' Cynthia had pleaded. 'You can't suppress the blacks in their own country for so long without something happening. You'll be murdered in your beds.' 'Oh Mother' Desmond had teased, 'You worry too much. Trust me. If there's any sign of trouble I promise Jemma will be on the first plane out.'

Yes there had been trouble at times, curfews and riots, but not the bloodbath everyone had anticipated and they were able to raise their family of three daughters in relative calm although Cynthia never could understand the complacency of the family living with apartheid as they did. 'It's no place to bring up the girls' she had often commented. 'They'll grow up spoilt and ignorant and with intolerable racist points of view'. 'No Mother' Jemma had responded. 'that won't be the case at all. Perhaps they will eventually play a part in undermining that attitude. Someone will have to do it someday. Don't be so negative!'

Cynthia's thoughts returned to the present. 'Come on girl' she coaxed, 'this is no time to be day dreaming!' Her glance fleetingly took in the four poster bed with its rose and cream patterned coverlet. The small mahogany bedside table now carried the latest editions of Harpers, Tatler, Vogue and other glossy magazines. In the centre of the room, surrounded by two armchairs was a large mahogany table on which she had carefully placed a cut glass crystal vase of flowers. A matching bowl of fresh fruit and a bottle of Perrier water completed the welcome. 'That's perfect' she nodded approvingly before checking the en-suite bathroom . Once satisfied that all was in order, Cynthia made her way down the long hall to the kitchen where Agnes worked away quietly humming to herself as she prepared the evening meal. 'The asparagus looks delicious' she commented. 'Everything is in order' Agnes reassured her noticing her worried frown. 'We've vichyssoise to start followed by new baby boiled potatoes, fresh asparagus, boiled ham, baby peas and a mixed salad.' 'Did we decide on strawberries or poached peaches in wine for dessert?' Lady Cynthia asked. 'I thought both' Agnes replied 'and Devonshire clotted cream if anyone wishes.' 'Perfect' Cynthia smiled. 'Perfect'.

By 4:00 p.m. Robert was settled in the drawing room nervously sipping on a large scotch. With Rebecca's arrival he felt uneasy, awkwardly greeting her, uncertain as to whether he should enfold her in his arms or whether to lightly kiss her on the cheek. Rebecca however had no doubt as to the way she expected him to respond. Grasping his hand in a firm but friendly manner, her warm smile quickly dissolved a few of Robert's fears. 'These are for you Lady Cynthia' Rebecca greeted her at the same time placing a large bouquet of flowers into her arms. 'Oh, they're really beautiful but you shouldn't have!' Cynthia scolded. 'Come and sit down my dear and have a drink. You must be extremely tired after such a long journey!' Rebecca nodded. She was extremely tired. The last week had eaten up so much of her energy. Aunt Anne had been marvellous once she had told her that she was going to spend the weekend with her Father but had made a point of reminding her of the promise to be absolutely honest with her once she returned to Roynick. But the most trying part over the last week had been Mark. 'You are going to take me to meet your parents when I return next week' she had insisted. He had finally relented, secretly hoping she would change her mind after her visit to London. The whole situation was completely out of control and no way could he imagine Rebecca feeling comfortable chatting with either of his parents or they with her, come to that! Each, he thought somewhat ironically, for their own reasons.

Chapter 15

REBECCA TOYED WITH the swizzle stick of her dry martini, the nervous gesture passing totally unnoticed by Cynthia or Robert Lawson. She looked so confident and poised Robert thought. Her hair was the deep auburn of her Mother also her pale unflawed complexion. But that was where the familiarity stopped. Her hazel eyes fringed with heavy lashes were frank and honest and her Romanesque nose gave the impression of a long lineage of past nobility. He smiled inwardly, 'That belongs to my part of the family' he reflected smugly. He had noticed that Rebecca was quite tall, taller than he had imagined her longs limbs partially covered by a pale blue cotton calf-length skirt. Robert found himself taking pride in the daughter facing him. A pride so great that he felt fit to burst.

'The drive wasn't too bad Rebecca answered.' 'Most of the journey was against the traffic, thank goodness!' Robert nodded. 'How's your Aunt Anne?' he asked politely. Rebecca slowly explained what had been happening in the House on the Hill. 'No doubt you wouldn't remember anything about it' she commented. Robert cleared his throat feeling a little threatened by an apparently innocent remark. 'Actually Rebecca I doubt that it has changed that much. As long as you are happy that's all that counts.' Rebecca stared at her Father. She desperately wanted to add that he had never bothered to enquire whether she was happy before and to ask why the sudden interest. But she hesitated, not wishing to offend Lady Cynthia. All these pent-up feelings and emotions could be released later. They had waited up until now. A few hours longer would make no difference at all she thought wryly.

'Let me show you to your room' Cynthia suggested rising from her chair. 'You may wish to have a rest for a while before freshening up for dinner. Agnes has prepared a delightful meal. 'You do like asparagus don't you?' 'I love it' Rebecca replied. 'By the way' Cynthia added, 'please call me Cynthia. All this Lady bit is too much to take sometimes although it does have its uses' she winked. Rebecca smiled. How lucky her Father was to have such a warm unaffected woman friend. Maybe he isn't as bad as he's been made out to be.

After a quick shower Rebecca had rested on her bed before changing into a silk two-piece Diana Fres outfit. She always travelled with one of these outfits in her weekend bag. No ironing, no fuss and they always looked bandbox fresh.

Prior to dinner Cynthia had shown her around the spacious apartment. Rebecca was genuinely impressed by its many beautiful rooms and the large roof garden with its pots of colourful plants. 'No one would ever believe how much space you have here,' Rebecca commented later. 'Yes' Cynthia smiled, 'appearances can be deceiving you know!'

Dinner was an unqualified success. Gradually the tension between Rebecca and her Father had eased and Robert congratulated himself on arranging the meeting in such amenable surroundings. By 11:00 p.m. Robert bade Cynthia and Rebecca a reluctant good night. 'I'll call by at 12 noon' he told Rebecca following their discussion earlier as to what they would do the following day. 'Perhaps we'll have lunch in Knightsbridge or somewhere else. Later the three of us will have dinner at Clarice's.'

Lying in her bed Rebecca felt completely exhausted and without a moment's hesitation fell into a deep sleep. The sound of someone gently knocking on her bedroom door awakened her with a start. For a brief moment she could not place where she was. 'I brought you a nice cup of tea my dear' Agnes greeted her. 'What time is it?' Rebecca asked, stifling a yawn. '8:30 No need to hurry. Just tell me what you would like for breakfast and I'll have it ready for you when you are up and about.' 'What about Lady Cynthia?' Rebecca asked. 'Oh her Ladyship is an early bird. She left a message that you must make yourself at home after leaving an hour ago. She will be back after mid-day. You're not going to be in for lunch I believe?' 'That's right' Rebecca replied, 'but I would love a poached egg on toast and another cup of tea for breakfast!'

Rebecca showered before dressing. The sun was shining and by all accounts, the day was going to be hot and humid. She dressed in a white cotton trouser suit, pale blue cotton three quarter sleeved blouse and white flat pumps. It was a comfortable but smart outfit and whatever her Father had planned, she felt adequately dressed.

Robert arrived on the dot of 12 noon. Rebecca greeted him in a more relaxed manner than that of the previous day. 'I thought we would have a quiet lunch at the China Garden,' he suggested. 'How do you feel about a Chinese meal?' Rebecca nodded her approval. She loved wanton soup and also spare- ribs. Over lunch Robert spoke more about his past and tried to explain a little as to what had occurred without delving too much into all the personal details.

Rebecca found her Father quite fascinating. Nothing like the person she had imagined him to be and underneath his debonair, man about town exterior, she detected more than a hint of tiredness. He spoke of his time with her Mother, stressing the fact that he was very young and immature. 'I'm sorry, I truly am that I never visited you but your Mother never forgave me for the way I treated her'. Rebecca understood. 'I married again' he continued, 'but they were disastrous times which I would prefer not to go into unless you really insist. I have a lot to be ashamed of I must confess!' Rebecca was beginning to see her Father in a different light. He admitted to having been a bit of a rogue but assured her he had now changed for the better especially, he confided, since he had been seeing Lady Cynthia. 'Aunt Anne mentioned she knows of her' Rebecca commented. 'Does she indeed!' Rebecca sensed a slight sarcasm in his tone. 'Well don't listen to everything anyone says!' he added quickly. 'Is she divorced?' Rebecca asked curiously. 'No, my dear, her husband died some years ago, poor chap. He was about 15 years her senior and I believe suffered a stroke. Now what have you been doing?' Rebecca described her small shop and many friends. She told him how badly she had felt as a young child not having her Father there when she needed him most. She explained her hurt and longing for a normal family life, and how, at times, she could not confide her deepest thoughts to her Mother. She wasn't quite sure whether to mention Mark, and then decided against it. Somehow it did not seem the right time or the right place.

By 3:30 p.m. Rebecca and her Father had talked a great deal of the past. Robert felt a genuine sadness that he had not been around over the years to share in her experiences. 'I do hope Rebecca that you will include me in at least a little of your future. I have missed so much of your past!'

Cynthia greeted Rebecca warmly on her return later that afternoon. She was too discreet to enquire if all had gone well but assumed by Rebecca's smile and relaxed manner that it had. 'Robert will collect us at 9:00 p.m.' Cynthia mentioned, 'so please do whatever you want.' 'I'd love to see some of your antiques if I may' Rebecca asked hesitantly. 'Of course you may' Cynthia enthused, happy that she could share her deep love with someone of the same interest.

Rebecca was in her element. Antique French clocks, small miniature figurines, a collection of old snuff boxes, exquisite Austrian and Czech perfume bottles and many other beautiful objet d'art filled the eye. Hand woven priceless Persian silk rugs scattered the highly lacquered polished wooden floor, an incredible Aladdin's cave, Rebecca thought. Everything was so beautifully kept, each piece holding its own story from the past. Wherever she looked there was something to catch her eye. 'They're wonderful!' Rebecca exclaimed, her eyes dancing with excitement and delight. 'My antiques in the shop fade next to these'. Cynthia nodded. 'They are splendid aren't they. I wouldn't part with any of them for the world. Each piece holds its own special memory! Each has a story from the past and it's a wonder they have survived. Whenever I pass an old antique shop or visit a vintage fair, I am always on the lookout for something very special hidden away amongst other items. You would be surprised at what I have found in the most unexpected places. Such a thrill to find something special, but unfortunately that does not happen as often as one would like!' Rebecca nodded. She had spent many hours wandering around old junk shops and fairs looking for that special item only to be disappointed on so many occasions. She had also written a short story about an elderly lady who collected perfume bottles and was hoping her niece would take care of her collection when she was no longer able to do so. 'Yes,' Rebecca sighed. 'That is one fantastic thing about living in the heart of London. There are so many antique shops to be explored. I never seem to have enough time to visit many of them when I am here!'

Chapter 16

A BUZZ OF excitement filled the atmosphere as the doorman greeted their arrival at Club Clarice. Robert had requested that a table in the Garden Room be reserved for dinner and as was customary, pre-dinner drinks were enjoyed in the beautiful reception lounge with its plush furnishings and ornate décor. Rebecca studied the menu carefully noticing the absence of the prices next to each item. 'Choose whatever you fancy.' Robert insisted. 'Everything is excellent and highly recommended!' He winked at Stafford, the head waiter, who was hovering nearby in preparation for their order. The menu was so varied and enticing that Rebecca was not quite sure what to choose, settling for scallops to start followed by rare prime Scottish beef, accompanied by fresh vegetables and a side salad.

Once seated at their table and enjoying dinner, Cynthia spoke about her children and grandchildren. Rebecca in turn told them about her spell at a girls' boarding school in Brighton and how she had loathed it so much that her Mother had eventually condescended to her leaving and attending a private day school nearer to home.

Having finished their meal they chatted over coffee and petite fours. 'How about a flutter' Robert suggested casually. 'I've never ever played at a casino' Rebecca admitted. 'Nothing to it my dear' her Father shrugged, 'just stay with me and I'll show you all the ropes!' Cynthia and Rebecca followed Robert as he made his way through the lounge and then up a small flight of stairs leading into another room. Guests were already grouped round various tables and the atmosphere was buzzing with excitement. Robert motioned Rebecca to join him at a roulette table. She sat intrigued by the amount of money being placed on various numbers and the excitement as one player scooped up a large win. Rebecca remembered the cuttings she had seen in the newspapers with all the gossip that her Father was losing more and more at the gaming tables. Just by chance she caught a glimpse of Cynthia handing her Father an envelope which appeared to be full of notes. She wished she hadn't. Somehow she knew it wasn't any of her business but she felt decidedly uneasy about the situation.

The following day was true to itself, a beautiful quiet Sunday. The sun shone brilliantly and the blue sky hardly wore a cloud. 'I thought we'd have a barbecue on the roof garden later this afternoon.' 'That's a perfect suggestion Cynthia' Robert enthused. He and Rebecca had wandered around Knightsbridge that morning gazing into the shop windows as they talked. Robert had spoken of his deep regard for Cynthia and hinted at the possibility of asking her to become his wife. 'She knows nothing of this' he confided, 'and anyway, I must somehow get my finances sorted out beforehand. Hopefully something will move on the Stock market soon! Fortune favours the brave!'

The barbeque had been great fun; the perfect way to spend the remainder of the perfect day. The unexpected arrival of Cynthia's son, David, added to the festivities. 'He obviously took a liking to Rebecca.' Robert commented later 'Perhaps they'll meet up again.' 'Perhaps' Cynthia hinted 'but I do hope so!'

Chapter 17

ANNE WAS INTRIGUED as Rebecca related the events of the weekend. It was apparent that she had enjoyed her stay in London and had got on well with her Father. 'Cynthia is a really delightful person' Rebecca enthused. 'I am sure you would like her very much.' 'I'm sure I would by all accounts' Anne agreed. 'I must admit it was a bit fraught with Father at first, but after our initial meeting, we got on quite well.' Anne nodded. She really wanted to ask a great many questions but thought it imprudent to do so. 'Did Robert speak a great deal of the past?' she prodded. 'Not exactly' Rebecca paused for a brief moment. 'He admitted that he had been immature and selfish at the time and I can understand a lot more now, especially how it must have been during the war. Cynthia related some of her experiences. How Lord Henry was away and the effect it had on their marriage. But he was nearly 16 years her senior which helped a great deal. Rebecca hesitated, 'you know what I mean, the fact that he was more mature, more, well reliable than Father.' Anne shook her head, 'You can't expect me to agree wholeheartedly Rebecca. I understand what you are saying but it is not really as simple as that.' Rebecca frowned. 'Obviously you were there but don't you think perhaps you could have been a little biased seeing as mummy was your sister?' Anne tried to hide her feelings of impatience and frustration. 'Let's not talk about it now my dear. It's all history and what counts is the present. All that really matters is your happiness and welfare. That is truly my only concern. I mean that Rebecca. Whatever happens in the future, my only thought is for your well-being'.

Rebecca rose from the large armchair and gently placed a kiss on the top of her Aunt's head. 'I know you care about me and I do appreciate you in every possible way. What I would have done without you I will never know. Oh, by the way, if I tell you a secret will you promise not to tell a soul. It's just between you and me.' 'Of course' Anne replied, eager to hear that it might be something to do with Rebecca's radiant glow over the last month or so. 'Father says he is thinking of proposing to Lady Cynthia. Isn't that marvellous! She's such a wonderful lady.' 'Yes I suppose that is', Anne replied, trying to hide the disappointment from her voice. 'He did say' Rebecca continued, 'that once his business had picked up financially he would pop the question but presently he's going through a bad patch!' 'Is that so' Anne murmured quietly. 'Is that so?'

The tone of Anne's voice immediately assured Charles that nothing drastic had taken place during Rebecca's long weekend away in London. 'I don't think there's anything to worry about right now' Anne whispered, 'but the best laid plans of mice and men!' 'I understand' Charles murmured. 'Shall we discuss it on Friday evening or do you need to see me before?' 'No Charles, not at all. I'll expect you for dinner at 7 p.m. on Friday then.' 'Yes my dear.' I look forward to seeing you.'

Tuesday was a busy day for Anne. She had arranged a coffee morning for a few friends to discuss ways of raising money for the local hospital. A bazaar was one suggestion. The ladies discussed what else they could do and finally decided on a raffle. 'I am sure we can find something very enticing Anne suggested, 'possibly the main prize could even be a short holiday somewhere exotic or a weekend of pampering in a local Spa.' Her friends agreed. With all their contacts a good raffle wouldn't be too difficult to arrange. 'Come on ladies' Anne jollied, 'let's tuck in to some of Molly's refreshments.'

Chapter 18

AGATHA BLAKE CAREFULLY wiped the cream work surface of the wooden kitchen table before placing three pairs of knives and forks in their customary setting. She had prepared a lamb stew for their evening meal and the appetising aroma filled every corner of the small kitchen. She glanced anxiously at the clock perched on the window ledge and hoped that for once Mark would be on time. He was always so busy now in his workshop that sometimes he would work late into the evening not realising the hours passing by.

Tom's voice called from the bottom of the stairs leading up to their tiny flat. 'I'm shutting up shop now. I'll be with you in ten minutes!' Agatha smiled, he's never changed. All these years and he still calls up the stairs before closing shop. They'd had a good life she reflected except for the war years. But she stopped herself thinking about then, the time in their lives when things hadn't been good. There was no room in her mind to think about then. It did no good. No good at all. Her eyes filled with tears. Tears that still needed to be shed but which had been bottled up for so long that once released would fill a river. 'No use fretting about the past' she scolded herself absent-mindedly dabbing her eyes with the damp dish cloth clutched tightly in her well worked hands. 'No use at all!'

Mark's cheery voice startled her 'My Lord, I nearly burned my tongue,' she scolded, carefully replacing the metal spoon next to the saucepan of bubbling stew. 'Smells good' Mark commented, humouring his Mother as was his way. 'And so it should! Only the best is in that pot, vegetables and all.' The sound of Tom's weary footsteps climbing the stairs was time to finish setting the remaining items on the table. From underneath a white starched teacloth she removed a large crusty loaf of bread which she placed on a square wooden bread board and into a plain pyrex dish she emptied some freshly boiled potatoes. Three large soup plates accommodated the steaming stew which was eaten with relish. 'Tastes good' Tom grunted. Mark nodded in agreement. Agatha watched with pleasure as the two men tucked in hungrily to their evening meal. Yes, they had a wonderful son in Mark and something to be thankful for. She was proud of his success in his workshop. It was good that he had decided not to join his Father. Tom had always made a living selling his newspapers, cigarettes, snuff, sweets and magazines, but that was not for Mark. Mark would always be able to stand on his own two feet, no matter what. Her eyes wandered over Tom's tired face. He was getting on in years now but nothing would stop him from opening up at 5:30 every morning to prepare the newspapers for early morning delivery. 'It would be like cutting off me right arm' he reproached Agatha every time she mentioned it as being too much for him. 'The day I stop working is the day you can get me tombstone ready.' Agatha would feel the cold shivers run up and down her spine at his words. Words she never wanted to hear, now or ever. So she had decided not to nag him any more hoping he knew best, but deep down realising full well he didn't. 'Men were all the same' she would mutter to herself, 'always knowing better until it was too late!' 'Come on woman' Tom's voice coaxed, 'eat up! You can't be daydreaming now. You've had all day for that.' Agatha looked at him reproachfully, but decided against saying anything in her own defence.

Tom settled down in the old armchair facing the television. He'd eaten well and when Mark was home he didn't waste time pretending to help in the kitchen. Anyway, that was woman's work and he wanted no part of it. He slowly fumbled with a small battered well-worn tin box which he kept on the side table next to his chair. The tobacco smelt good, he thought to himself, as he carefully rolled his own skinny cigarette. He glowered at it, knowing that it was something he shouldn't be doing but he was too old to break the habit of a lifetime now. 'It's got to stop!' Doctor Jones would chastise him. 'It will kill you soon Tom. It's got to stop!' But it hadn't stopped. The only concession he'd made to the warning was to roll them thinner. 'Short and skinny' he'd joked, 'that's the way I like 'em now, short and skinny.' Even so, he was still out of breath climbing the comparatively short flight of stairs leading up from the shop below. His heart attack had put the fear of God in him. He admitted that, but nine years had passed since then and he was still alive and kicking. 'So much for Doctor Jones and my cigarettes' he thought smugly inhaling the putrid smoke. Deep down he knew the doctor was right but he would never admit it to anyone, especially to Agatha.

Mark immersed his strong broad hands into the hot bubbly washing up water at the same time watching his Mother from the corner of his eye. He was looking for the right moment to speak but had to admit to himself that no moment was going to be right for what he had to say.

'Ma' he stammered, 'there's something I've been wanting to ask you.' 'Yes, what is it son?' she asked, a slight note of apprehension entering her voice. 'You remember my telling you about Rebecca?' Mark felt the heat rising beneath his skin prickling with embarrassment. 'I'd like to bring her home on Sunday afternoon!' Agatha looked at him in total disbelief. 'You what!' she spluttered, her mouth open wide in amazement, 'You want to bring her here!' 'Yes Ma, I do.' 'Whatever for?' 'She wants to meet you and Dad, Ma, that's all!' 'Why should she be wanting to do that son? Anyway I don't want to meet her!' Mark stammered, 'because we're seeing one another.' 'I know that' his Mother retorted 'but you told me there was nothing in it and, remember I told you she's not for you. Have you forgotten?' 'No Ma, I hadn't forgotten but' he hesitated, 'but she still wants to meet you.' Agatha remained silent. This was a thunderbolt out of the blue and she felt as though she had been struck by lightning. She'd heard so much gossip about the folks from the big house on the hill and some of it she never believed. She remembered Jack and Mary Henderson, Rebecca's grandparents. How proper they were, proud too and never mixing with anyone except their own kind. Their daughters were the same. Well perhaps not the youngest but the older one was too full of her own self-importance when she was small. All puffed up and that. Agatha could see her now, stamping her little foot if she had to wait in line. A proper little miss she was and always shouting at her younger sister to hurry up. She'd always felt sorry for the younger lass. How she would blink away the tears, too proud to let them roll down her hot flushed little cheeks. And now her son wanted to bring one of them home here. Agatha nodded her head in dismay. 'Did I hear right?' she questioned Mark, 'You want to bring Rebecca home here?' 'Yes Ma' Mark answered quietly. 'There'll be no fuss, she just wants to be with us the way we are.' 'And why should I be fussing son?' Agatha remarked, a trace of sarcasm entering her voice. 'She'll not be the Queen of England you know!' Mark sighed. 'I knew you'd make it difficult. I told her I didn't want her to come.' 'Oh!' Agatha replied tartly, 'so you didn't think we'd be good enough eh? Well son, we're as good as the next and even better come to that. Just because we haven't got a fancy car or a big fancy house, doesn't mean we're not good people. Money doesn't mean everything son.' Mark nodded. There was no point trying to reason. All he ended up doing was to go round in circles. 'Tom' Agatha's voice called, 'Can you come in here!' 'What is it?' Tom replied impatiently. Muttering under his breath, Tom reluctantly returned to the small kitchen. He knew there was trouble but what it could be he had not the vaguest idea. 'Your son wants to bring Rebecca here on Sunday afternoon.' Tom returned her gaze, his face a complete blank. 'Well.' Agatha urged him, 'What do you say to that?' 'Nothing' he grunted. 'Nothing' Agatha exclaimed, 'Surely you can say something.' Tom stared at them both, totally puzzled as to why he was in the centre of all this hoo ha. Mark had brought girlfriends home before so what was Agatha going on about now. 'Who's Rebecca?' he asked. 'Good Lord Tom, wake up. It's the Henderson's granddaughter from the House on the Hill and I don't want her here!' 'Don't be so bloody foolish woman,' Tom chided. 'Of course she can come here. Now stop fussing and let me watch my television in quiet!' Agatha continued to busy herself in the kitchen. 'So it's all right Ma?' Mark questioned tentatively. 'You'll like her Ma, I know you will.' Agatha shook her head. 'Well son, don't say I didn't warn you and not for the first time either. She's not for you son. I feel it in my bones. She's not for you!'

Chapter 19

REBECCA CAREFULLY CLOSED the drawer of her writing bureau into which she had placed a letter thanking her Father for their week-end in London. She had also arranged for a large bouquet of flowers to be delivered to Lady Cynthia in appreciation of her stay.

Glancing at her watch she hurried downstairs to join Charles Matthews and her Aunt for dinner. 'I gather you enjoyed your week-end in London' Charles Matthews commented, fumbling with the cellophane wrapper of his favourite Davidoff cigar. 'Yes I did' Rebecca replied. 'It was strange meeting my Father after so many years but I'm pleased now that I have actually seen and talked with him.' Charles nodded. He remembered Robert Lawson quite well. Not that he'd ever had much reason to spend time with the man, nor Robert Lawson with him, come to that. He vaguely remembered his being the second born son of Lord William Lawson and as such, never receiving a hereditary title. He also recollected that upon Lord William's death there was talk of the family wealth being somewhat depleted, ploughed into his nursing care due to the onset of arterial sclerosis. Charles Matthews shook his head acknowledging the memories which had, until now, remained dormant. How a seemingly perfectly healthy man could have been betrayed in his later years by an illness which took away his pride and well-being. How the gradual but increasing loss of memory spared him a lot of anguish but how heavily the family bore the strain and how during the years leading to his total incontinence the family resigned themselves to his impending death.

'Yes, I do remember your Father' he added, 'but I must admit I never knew him well!' Anne glanced nervously at Charles wondering whether Rebecca would mention any further events of her stay. 'How's Gerald?' Rebecca asked, abruptly changing the subject. She hadn't seen Gerald since their dinner party and apart from a few phone calls to friends hadn't seen any of them either. Her absence had caused a certain amount of comment but she hadn't felt inclined to tell them about her meetings with Mark. Not even her Aunt. But she had promised herself that once her meeting with Mark's parents was over then would be the right time. She smiled inwardly. This coming Sunday, Mark had promised to take her home. It was strange really. There was no need for her to feel nervous at her impending visit, but she was. Whenever her thoughts strayed to him and his family, butterflies fluttered around in her stomach over which she had no control. 'What were you thinking about my dear?' Anne questioned. 'Oh nothing, nothing really; Nothing of importance,'

Rebecca answered, slightly flustered. Anne watched her niece. She longed for Rebecca to confide in her but knew she had to bide her time. 'Would you like a cup of coffee, Charles?' Anne suggested. 'No thank you my dear, it keeps me awake. The brandy will do nicely thank you.' 'I've given Jenny the day off tomorrow,' Rebecca informed her Aunt 'so I'll be making an early start.' The only start I'll be making tomorrow,' Charles Matthews joked, 'will be on the golf course.' Anne sighed. 'I wish I could find it in me to play. Since my wretched back started acting up I haven't as much as looked at my clubs. Did you know that in an article I was reading, it stated that golf is the culprit for many a ruined back? Fortunately I've got my bridge to keep me occupied but it's not the same as an outdoor sport.' Charles patted her hand condescendingly, 'We've more wet days than dry ones so it would seem, so there's no need to feel too badly. It could be worse Anne, so just be grateful for what you have!' 'I am Charles, I truly am' she replied, glancing at Rebecca. 'I've a great deal to be thankful for, I truly realise that!'

Chapter 20

REBECCA CANTERED ACROSS the soggy fields. The previous evening the heavens had opened up and Sunday morning was total devastation. 'You'll not be riding in this?' Molly reproached Rebecca as she settled down to an early breakfast dressed in her riding habit. 'I won't be out long' she reassured her, tucking into fried eggs bacon and hot toast. 'I'll be back after an hour.' 'I should think so too' Molly added, 'you'll be catching a death of cold in weather like this. I don't see why you have to go out at all.' 'Oh Molly, do stop fussing. There's nothing for you to worry about. A little rain won't hurt me or Ruby.' Molly tutted to herself as she prepared a large pot of tea. Why Rebecca couldn't stay at home in this weather she could not understand for the life of her. She tutted to herself again quietly, whilst absent-mindedly nodding her head as she poured herself a second cup of tea.

The outline of a car slowly weaving its way along the narrow winding lane was cause for Rebecca to gently pull on Ruby's reins, bringing her to a slow halt. 'What a lousy morning' Mark greeted Rebecca, jumping out of his grey Morris Minor. Rebecca stood facing him at the same time holding on to Ruby's reins. She felt the same exhilaration which she always felt on seeing him once more. His arms opened wide to hug her and she laughed as the now light rain sprinkled their faces as they embraced. 'Oh Mark, I so missed you!' 'I missed you too!' Mark replied a little self-consciously. 'Well' Rebecca coaxed, after they had embraced once more, 'what did your Mother say about my coming over today?' Mark was aware of the note of defiance in Rebecca's voice challenging him not to have remembered her last words before leaving for her stay in London. 'Well?' she asked pointedly. 'Everything's arranged' Mark answered abruptly, dreading the afternoon meeting and wishing it were over. 'Can you meet me at Copse Corner at 3.30 and you can follow me in your car from there.' 'Great!' Rebecca exclaimed, jumping up to hug him warmly. 'I knew you wouldn't let me down! I knew you wouldn't!' Mark grinned back at her forgetting for a brief moment the comments of his Mother over the last week and her incessant pessimistic remarks.

Rebecca hurried home happy in the knowledge that she was reaching a turning point in their relationship. Soon she thought to herself, soon we'll be able to see more of each other. We'll go to dinner or to a film. Soon I'll show Mark everything that's near and dear to me. Soon everything will fall into place.' Handing Ruby over to Arthur for a good rub down, Rebecca made her way to the kitchen. 'You see Molly I told you I wouldn't be long!' Molly eyed Rebecca curiously, how alive she was and so happy. As if a new world was opening up for her, as if......'It's strange' she told Arthur later, 'first Miss Henderson with all those meetings with that Mr. Matthews and now Miss Rebecca running around like a wild fawn. It's very strange Arthur!' 'There you go again' Arthur teased. 'If it's not one thing you'll be worrying about, then it's another. My goodness, what will you be telling me next! Pigs could fly, I wouldn't wonder!'

Rebecca lay on her bed deep in thought. Every inch of her body felt alive with an excitement that even a hot bath had been unable to subdue. She felt so deliriously happy. So very happy and she so desperately wanted it to last. The meeting with her Father had proved beyond her wildest dreams to be a success. No bitterness or recriminations. Only feelings of forgiveness and disappointment at opportunities missed. Even Aunt Anne, whom she loved dearly, had come up trumps. And now to top it all there was Mark. Someone whom she inexplicably had very deep and warm feelings for that she found difficult to understand. Of course she had heard of love at first sight occurring between the most unlikely of people. Now it had, by some strange quirk of fate, happened to her. She was unable to explain it. Unable to explain the tenderness and pleasure, the longing and overwhelming feelings of caring and feeling loved. She felt at peace with herself and with the world in general. Life was strange but whatever it was that had brought her and Mark together, she intended to nurture it despite the great divide in their backgrounds and upbringing. A triviality of no consequence she reassured herself.

She dried her rich auburn hair allowing it to fall naturally around her slender shoulders. Her reflection in the mirror radiated happiness and consequently she had never looked lovelier. It was going to be a difficult afternoon, she knew that but she was confident at winning Mark's parents over, of that she had no doubt!

Chapter 21

AGATHA GREETED REBECCA a little stiffly. 'Come in lass. Come in and make yourself comfortable.' Tom dragged his aching body out of his chair. His wife had made him dress up in his one and only three piece navy suit which had last seen the light of day at his sister's husband's funeral three years back. A stale odour of mothballs was causing his eyes to itch and the buttoned down waistcoat hadn't allowed for the extra bit of weight which now covered his once rakishly thin body. 'Hello lass' he greeted Rebecca giving her a sly wink. Rebecca smiled. She felt an affinity towards this man with his genuine lack of self-consciousness. 'Me wife's been busy flapping around all day waiting for you,' he whispered in her ear. Mark looked on awkwardly. Their flat had always been small but he had never really noticed it before. Not even when they had occasional visits from relatives or friends. Today, however, he was virtually suffocating from its closeness. He unloosened his tie and fidgeted with the cream coloured lace tablecloth. 'Why don't you sit here?' Tom motioned to Rebecca.

She sat down in a smaller armchair close to his. Tom studied her face taking in her beautiful rich auburn hair which surrounded her pale small face. He looked at her carefully, a slight lump coming to his throat as his mind wandered back in time. She was a pretty lass, he acknowledged that and he was proud of his son in recognising such a lovely creature. But somehow her face reminded him of someone he once knew and loved and it bothered him. 'Can you pass me that tin?' he asked Rebecca pointing to the table now nearer to her than to him. Tom slowly rolled a cigarette, his fingers gradually ceasing to tremble. 'I'll expect you'll be wanting a nice cup of tea!' Agatha exclaimed, placing a large teapot now covered with a bright yellow tea cosy onto a place mat on the dining room table. 'Mark told me you like Cornish pasties so I've made some for today' she added proudly 'and you might like to try my home made cake and biscuits!' 'Thank you' Rebecca replied, 'but you shouldn't have gone to so much trouble.' If only they would all relax, she thought to herself, their tensions communicating to her. 'Did Mark tell you he can now ride my mare Ruby?' she asked, trying to take their attention off her for a while but then regretting her words. Agatha's face registered surprise. 'That he did not' she answered curtly, inwardly hurt that he had been keeping things from her. 'Oh Ma!' Mark interrupted, 'You know how you are about horses. If I'd have told you, you'd not have liked it. You're always saying it's too dangerous and not for common folk.' 'Who spoke about common folk?' Agatha's eyes burned with anger, 'You and your funny ideas!' Tom's voice brought her ranting to a halt. 'I knew of your grandparents' he interrupted, turning to Rebecca. 'Fine upstanding people they were too. You can be proud of them lass, that you can.' Rebecca looked surprised. 'I don't remember them too well' she confided, 'but I know they worked hard and eventually bought the land that is now ours.' 'Shrewd they were' Tom continued, enjoying his sojourn into the past. 'There were nought round these parts then.' he continued. 'No village with shops and all those places to eat. No, it was a different world then and better for it.' 'Did you meet your wife here then?' Rebecca asked. Tom grinned. 'Well not exactly. Agatha lived some way away but I knew a good thing when I saw it.' Rebecca noticed the slight flush which crept into Agatha's cheeks, softening her tense features. 'So I courted and married her and brought her here and this is where we've been ever since.' 'I remember your Mother and Aunt when they were small too' Agatha added. 'Your ma was not so easy that I remember, always bossing her sister around!' 'Ma', Mark interrupted, embarrassed by the conversation, 'that's nothing to do with Rebecca. Don't go on so.' Rebecca turned her attention to Mark. 'I love hearing stories from the past and how my Mother was when she was small. Please tell me all you remember, I do so want to hear!' Agatha and Tom were in their element. They had never expected the afternoon to be so informal and full of old times; so many memories to be disturbed and talked over and so much in the past to be spoken of and remembered once more.

'I really enjoyed myself.' Agatha confided in Rebecca later, 'You've brought back so many memories, that you have. It's really been a pleasure having you here.' 'And I've enjoyed myself too' Rebecca smiled, 'and you do make the best homemade Cornish pasties I have ever tasted.' Agatha's face glowed with pride. 'Aye Tom' she explained later, 'our Mark's got a good eye for a lovely lass.' Tom grunted, 'She is that' but deep down something was troubling him. Something he could not put his finger on, but not for the moment anyway.

Rebecca heaved a quiet sigh of relief as she finally bade her farewell. 'Next time you will come to visit us' she told Mark before leaving. He sighed too. It had been a very tense afternoon for him and he was thankful it was over. Rebecca had really been so tactful with his parents and it had been quite surprising watching his Mother warm to her as they chatted away about the past. 'She's a nice lass' Agatha had told him later that evening before retiring to bed.

Chapter 22

Once back home Rebecca re-read the letter which she had written to her Father. Before sealing the envelope she had added a post script. 'By the way' she wrote in her perfect neat handwriting, 'I didn't tell you before that I have met someone here that I really do think a great deal of. His name is Mark. Perhaps I will be able to tell you more about him next time I come to London.

Love, Rebecca'

MONDAY MORNING WAS the usual rush. She had decided to tell her Aunt about Mark over dinner and hoped the following Sunday Mark would agree to tea at the House on the Hill. It was with a little trepidation that Rebecca broached the subject that evening. 'Aunt Anne, I have someone I would like you to meet'. Anne tried hard to hide her surprise she knew Gerald and Rebecca's other friends, so who could she possibly want her to meet. 'His name's Mark and he lives in the village'.

Anne was completely taken off guard. 'Did you say he lives in the village?' 'Yes', Rebecca replied defensively. 'I do hope that won't make any difference?' 'Of course not' Anne answered truthfully. 'Of course not, my dear, why should it?' 'Well' Rebecca hesitated, 'he isn't like Gerald or Miles or any of my friends. He's completely different. I can't really explain but he is special Aunt Anne but I do so want you to meet him!' Anne stared at Rebecca. 'How strange,' she thought, 'how strange that Rebecca had met someone in the village and obviously not of the same social background. Her thoughts once more turned to Sam. He had been on her mind so much of late and now, here was Rebecca in her own way mimicking her own past. Well I won't stand in her way, local boy or not. History had a strange way of repeating itself, but this time it was not going to. If Rebecca feels a great deal for this young man, sobeit. Her Mother's voice from the past echoed in her ears. 'Why don't you find yourself a good looking young man like your sister?' Suddenly all the humiliation engulfed her once more. The hurting so badly that she felt the wounds would open up revealing to everyone the pain and torment she was feeling inside. And then came the war years and poor Sam. He never lived to see his beautiful daughter. A daughter he would have been so proud of. A daughter........she stopped herself. There was no point in all these memories, that was then and this is now. There was no reason to believe that Rebecca had any intention of wishing to marry Mark. As she said, he was a friend and she was bringing him home for tea.

It was a compliment that Rebecca wished her to meet him. And she would. 'I'd be delighted to meet Mark' Anne exclaimed. 'Yes, I am really looking forward to it very much indeed!'

Chapter 23

THE PERFUMED ENVELOPE and the neat handwriting brought a smile to Robert Lawson's eyes. Since Rebecca's stay in London he had become a virtual teetotaller and was beginning to feel the pangs of withdrawal. Not that he had the shakes or cravings. It was just the overwhelming boredom. It wasn't the booze, he admitted to himself, it was the gambling. How the adrenalin flowed with the last couple of hundred pounds riding on a few numbers of the roulette wheel. But something sadistic and strange was also taking hold. He was finding more than ever an excitement in losing more than winning. He would hold his own post mortem late into the early hours of the morning whilst lying on his bed. Where he should have covered the board and how much he would have won if that blasted croupier had not decided to change over shift just at the critical point. Sometimes Cynthia had been with him but as a sexual object the table was his only real drive. It sapped his emotions to such a point that no woman, not even the sexiest bitch on God's earth would have been able to compete.

He read his daughter's letter slowly before replacing it in the envelope which he left on the breakfast table alongside the customary mounting bills which he had not bothered so much as to look at.

'I received a letter from Rebecca this morning' he told Cynthia later. 'She sends her love and hopes to see you again soon!' 'That's very nice' Cynthia commented. She had really taken to Rebecca and in her mind had already begun to think of ways to bring David and Rebecca together. 'She's mentioned some chap by the name of Mark' Robert mumbled. 'Strange that. She never said a word when she was here. I wonder why?' Cynthia laughed. 'Oh Robert, don't take on so. He can't be that important otherwise she would have mentioned him before. Anyway we've our own plans for her and David. The quicker we have her back here for another stay, the better!' Cynthia was right of course. Whoever this Mark chap was, he had other plans for his daughter. He also had plans for Cynthia too, but these involved a cash flow problem. If only he could borrow a couple of grand. Well at least forty. He anticipated spending around twenty thousand on a ring. Through some contacts in the trade it would be worth far, far more. The remainder would provide respectability for a month or so. He made a mental note to call Rebecca the next morning. It was too short notice for her to join them this coming week-end but perhaps the one after. Obviously he was aware of the Trust Fund also the fact that Rebecca must have put quite a bit away over the years. She was a sensible careful girl. No flies on her.

Well what did he expect? She was a chip off the old block, no doubt about that. 'What if I ask her down for the weekend after next?' Robert suggested. 'That would be lovely!' Cynthia enthused. 'It would also give me the chance to ensnare David. 'Yes, do that Robert. What a good idea!'

The next morning Robert called Rebecca. 'Gosh it's such a surprise to hear from you' Rebecca told him truthfully. 'Did you receive my letter?' 'It so happens I did but Cynthia and I wondered if you would come and stay the week-end after next?' Rebecca hesitated a moment before replying. 'I'm not sure really' she hesitated again. 'Rebecca I would not be so persistent under normal circumstances, but you no doubt will remember our chat, the confidential one.' 'Yes' she added excitedly. 'Well it concerns that and something else. I do need to talk to you privately' he whispered, 'please say yes'. 'Under the circumstances of course I'll come but this time I'd like to arrive on the Saturday. Is that O.K?' 'That's fine' Robert replied. 'I knew you would come. That's my girl. That is really good news!'

Chapter 24

MOLLY HAD BEEN in a dither all morning. She was used to Rebecca bringing her friends home and even preparing dinner parties and the likes, unless Rebecca insisted on taking care of them herself. But this Sunday was special somehow. She could sense an air of expectancy. Miss Henderson had made a point of checking what she was serving for tea and Rebecca had also popped in and out of the kitchen at various intervals checking this and that. Something she was not prone to do normally. As it was a pleasant summer's day, Molly had suggested that perhaps tea in the garden would be a lovely idea. 'I think I'd prefer it indoors' Rebecca had replied. 'Aunt Anne doesn't like sitting out if it is too warm!' 'I take it you won't be taking Ruby for a ride then this morning?' 'No Molly, not today but perhaps early this evening. We'll see!'

It had been a strange morning. Rebecca definitely had butterflies in her stomach but for the life of her she couldn't understand why. Why was she so worried about Mark and Aunt Anne's meeting? It wasn't the first time she had brought a friend on his own home. She was being foolish behaving more like a girl in her teens than a young woman of her age. At 3:00 p.m. Rebecca drove her small mini to Copse Corner where she had arranged to meet Mark. The arrangement was that he would meet her there and then follow her in his car to the House on the Hill.

She waited anxiously until she finally saw his car slowly meandering towards her. 'I thought you were never coming!' she exclaimed nervously. 'I'm sorry but Dad came over a little strange so I waited to see that he was all right.' Rebecca looked genuinely concerned. 'He's been feeling a bit off colour since your visit but he refuses to see Doctor Jones.' 'Why ever not' Rebecca asked. 'Well he's stubborn and says all the doctor will say is that he should give up smoking! Doctor Jones has wanted him to stop for a long time now!' 'Are you sure you want to come Mark. I really would understand if you'd prefer to go home.' 'No that's all right, I just won't stay too long if you don't mind.'

Molly had set a small table in Miss Henderson's sitting room. She had carefully prepared dainty sandwiches, a bowl of plump strawberries with whipped cream and had also taken the opportunity to bake some of her special shortbread biscuits and a deliciously tempting apple tart. Two French windows opened out onto the patio which was now ablaze with colour. The sound of approaching cars on the gravel outside alerted Molly to Rebecca's arrival.

'Arthur, you'll never believe who Miss Rebecca's brought home for tea.' 'Who?' Arthur asked, curious at the mounting excitement in his wife's voice. 'It's Agatha and Tom's son. That's who!' 'She's what!' Arthur spluttered, practically choking on his tea. 'Agatha and Tom's son' Molly repeated, 'you know, the Blacks!' 'Well I'll be darned' Arthur muttered, a look of amazement covering his face. 'What on earth would she be doing with him?' 'Your guess is as good as mine!' Molly replied sarcastically. 'She shouldn't be mixing with them folks. She should be with her own.' Arthur for once, lost for words, nodded his head in total agreement.

Mark's eyes took in the grandness of the House on the Hill. It was so imposing, so large, so grand and so much bigger than he could ever have imagined. The beautiful winding staircase, the airy entrance hall with its numerous heavy oak panelled doors leading to, he knew not where left him with the feeling of an imposter. He felt gawky, gauche and out of place, as if he didn't belong. To add to that he had caught a glimpse of a middle aged grey haired woman in a starched white pinafore eyeing him curiously from behind one of the partially open doors. 'Come on Mark' Rebecca coaxed, gently taking hold of his arm. 'You look as though you have seen a ghost.' Mark forced a weak smile. 'It's so big here' the words tumbled from his mouth. 'I never thought a home could be so grand, so ….' 'Oh Mark' Rebecca teased, 'you don't notice it after a while. It isn't so grand or large really. Come on, I'll show you round the gardens before Aunt Anne joins us for tea.'

Anne had been lying on her bed, a cool flannel pressed to her forehead when she heard the arrival of Rebecca and Mark. It had been an exceptionally humid morning and once the storm came to clear the air, so she would feel more human again. She loathed the oppressive heat. The feeling of being enveloped by the very air one breathed. Storm weather she had always called it, but there was no point in taking aspirin or any other type of medication. Nature would take care of it in its own way and as soon as the dark clouds began their formidable slow cantankerous rumblings, then she would gradually regain her own self-composure feeling the freedom of space around her. Muttering under her breath at the inopportune time to be feeling unwell, she carefully combed her hair and re-applied some lipstick to her lips, dabbing a little rouge to her pallid cheeks. She had been looking forward to this meeting a little apprehensively perhaps, but there again, she reproached herself Mark must have been feeling somewhat nervous too!

The sound of Rebecca and Mark's voices drifted towards her from the sitting room. Her head still felt somewhat fuzzy but she tried to dismiss it with the shrug of her shoulders. On entering the sitting room, Rebecca jumped up to greet her. Anne's eyes slowly focused on Mark and at the same time she felt her body tense and her head became a swimming pool of blackness. 'My God!' Rebecca exclaimed, 'My God, Aunt Anne's fainted!'

The strong putrid odour of smelling salts thrust under her nose, gradually awakened Anne's senses. Molly's and Rebecca's face gradually cleared from their blurred images swimming around in her head. 'Are you feeling any better?' Molly asked at the same time pressing a cold glass of water to Anne's dry lips. 'Yes thank you' Anne whispered. 'You did give us a start!' Rebecca consoled her Aunt, a worried expression written across her face. 'Thank goodness you didn't knock your head as you fell. If it hadn't been for Mark......' 'Where is he?' Anne interrupted. 'He's in my sitting room' Rebecca responded. Anne nodded. 'I'm so sorry Rebecca. I've spoilt your day!' 'Don't be silly, of course you haven't. Anyway, if it makes you feel any better Mark's Father has been taken poorly too and Mark really would have preferred not to have come today. It seems as if we chose the wrong day then, doesn't it?' Anne nodded her head weakly. 'You know my dear I think I'd like to lie down on my bed for a while'.

'You should have seen her Arthur' Molly prattled on, 'it was as if she'd seen a ghost, she was that white!' The sound of thunder accompanied by a torrential downpour of rain stopped any further conversation in its tracks. 'Let's be closing the windows quickly now. This rain will bring us all relief. Miss Henderson was right as usual.' 'She always is' Molly replied. 'Always is when it's storm weather.'

The summer storm had finally cleared the air bringing with it the smell of fresh wet grass mingled with the heady scents of summer flowers. Life in the

House on the Hill was once more at peace, or so it would seem. Anne now recovered from her attack was occupied with her fund raising for the local hospital while Rebecca was busy with her shop. 'I'm going to London on Saturday,' she told Jenny. 'Aunt Anne is fine now, thank goodness. Doctor Jones gave her another thorough examination yesterday and apart from being a little highly strung, which he said was nothing to worry about, apparently she is in perfect health.' 'That must be a great relief to you' Jenny replied. 'Enjoy your stay in London. Perhaps you will be able to find some nice things whilst you are there.'

Anne had offered no objections to Rebecca's news that she would be seeing her Father once more. 'There are a few things he would like to discuss and I think it is concerning Lady Cynthia'. Anne had smiled. If Robert was seriously thinking of marrying the woman, then there would be no danger financially for Rebecca. After all the events of the last weeks, that in itself was good news. But she had much more pressing matters on her mind. Matters which were causing her deep distress and anxiety until she finally had an opportunity to lay them to rest.

Chapter 25

'I NEVER REALISED how tense I was' Rebecca confided in Cynthia over tea. 'It's been an awful time since I was here last. Aunt Anne fainting was so unusual and gave us a nasty shock!' 'I can well imagine' Cynthia replied sympathetically, 'but you can relax here my dear. The only person visiting this week-end apart from your Father, of course, is my son David. You remember him don't you? We're having a casual late lunch tomorrow and there is a possibility I may have to drag your Father out for an hour or so. He doesn't like the idea but we should visit a mutual friend in hospital. He loathes hospitals. Did you know that your Father has a sort of ostrich syndrome when it comes to matters relating to one's health? He'll have to get over it one of these days for I'd hate to see him ill at any time, heaven forbid!'

'I've been dying to hear your news' Rebecca remarked to her Father once they were alone. 'Well I hope you'll approve' Robert winked, squeezing Rebecca's arm affectionately. 'I've decided to ask Cynthia to marry me. Unfortunately' he hesitated, 'unfortunately it isn't as simple as it would appear!' Rebecca eyed her Father curiously across the small coffee table which looked out onto the busy street of Knightsbridge. Weekend shoppers dogged the pavements and the noise of the constant stream of traffic was tempered by the enclosed surroundings and the gentle music being played in the background. 'I do need to borrow some money' Robert admitted. 'Around £40,000 in fact, but there would be a guarantee of repayment once everything is settled.' Rebecca remained silent. She did have the money her Father required and she certainly had no need for it at the present time. Even if she never saw a penny of it again in her lifetime, it wouldn't make the slightest difference. She had long accepted the fact that she was a wealthy woman in her own right and besides, Robert was her Father and that was all that really mattered. She had also accepted the fact that her parents were obviously ill suited and was aware of the infringements that her Mother had imposed on her Father. But all those things were in the past. This was now, the present, the future and it was her decision, hers alone. 'Don't worry Father' she smiled encouragingly, 'you can pop the question whenever you wish. On Monday I'll arrange for the money to be transferred to your account in London. I'm so happy for you Father, I really am!' Robert looked at her, an amazed expression covering his tired features. Suddenly he felt all the worries lifting from his broad shoulders. 'You are a chip off the old block, you really are. Thank you Rebecca, from the bottom of my heart.'

Evening was a light hearted and happy affair. Dinner at Clarices lived up to its usual expectations and the roulette wheel offered a condescending win. By 1:00 tired and ready to leave, they were about to climb into the chauffeur driven limousine when the flash bulb of a hidden camera intruded on their privacy. 'Those bloody snoopers!' Robert growled, seething with anger. 'Oh Robert, do calm down' Cynthia pleaded. 'Why should you worry about a stupid photographer'? 'Yes Father, Cynthia's right!' Robert shrugged his shoulders. Under normal circumstances he would have chased the bastard and smashed his snooping camera to smithereens. But this was one time where he had no option but to swallow his pride. Monday morning the gossip column in the Daily Time would no doubt carry their picture and then no doubt sold off to the glossies. 'At least I wasn't pissed' he thought ruefully.

David arrived in good time for Sunday lunch. The barbecue was soon under way and Rebecca and David chatted amiably, engrossed in one another's conversation. 'Don't you mind being on your own?' Rebecca asked. 'Yes I do' David replied truthfully, 'but until, if ever, I meet the right person that's how it's going to be. What about you?' Rebecca blushed, 'Well I am quite involved with someone. Robert has never met him but I did take him home to meet Aunt Anne but she promptly fainted on the spot!' David grinned. 'Was he that bad?' David joked, the two of them falling into fits of laughter. 'What's so funny' Robert and Cynthia enquired. 'Oh, nothing really, nothing at all, just a private joke!' Cynthia gave Robert a discreet nudge. 'I'm so sorry darling' she addressed David, 'but Robert and I must disappear for an hour or so. We explained to Rebecca yesterday that we had to leave for a short while today. Would you mind awfully David?' David sensed that this was some sort of devious plot but for Rebecca's sake refrained from saying so. Rebecca may not have seen through his Mother's little plot but she couldn't pull the wool over his eyes. He knew the machinations of her mind only too well. 'Of course not Mother' he reassured her. 'Don't worry about a thing. We will be fine!'

David had to admit that the remainder of the afternoon had been very pleasant. Rebecca was so different from the women he normally spent time with also much younger too. Living in the country she had an air of softness about her, an indefinable quality of innocence and purity. Yes she was refreshingly different and he was quite grateful to his Mother for her little games. This time he was very grateful indeed! Rebecca was aware of David's intense gaze. 'Is anything wrong?' David shrugged, non-committedly. 'Sorry, I was miles away. Are you coming down next week-end?' 'No' Rebecca replied. 'I only came down this week because I needed to spend some time with Father. My friend Mark and I haven't seen much of each other lately and I do miss him!' 'Oh!' David's face registered disappointment. 'Well let me know in advance for next time. Perhaps we can take in the theatre. Just as friends' he added quickly, noting the troubled look which fleetingly crossed her brow. 'Why don't you put this somewhere where it won't get lost?' Rebecca carefully placed the small cream gold embossed card in her purse. 'I won't lose it' she added, 'I promise.' David smiled. He had no intention of letting her get away from him that easily. Whoever this Mark fellow was, he was ready to fight him by any means possible, hand tooth and nail if need be.

Driving back to Roynick, Rebecca reflected how well events had been falling into place. She was so very happy at the thought of her Father's forthcoming marriage. David was nice she admitted to herself. He was easy to be with and to talk to. She looked forward to seeing him again and was already planning to introduce him to one or two of her unattached friends. As far as the money transfer was concerned, she was a little hesitant at explaining this to her Aunt. But there again was it really necessary to do so?

Once more on approaching the House on the Hill, she was happy to be home and happy to be seeing Mark again. She had planned to meet him at his workshop the following day. An event she was looking forward to with great anticipation.

Chapter 26

ANNE HAD BEEN relieved to hear Rebecca finally starting up the engine of her blue mini for the drive to Cynthia and her Father in London. She had bid her farewell with the usual note of caution to drive carefully. Checking herself once more in the tall wardrobe mirror, she was quite satisfied that her appearance was one of simplicity rather than one of wealth! It was essential, she told herself, that on such a visit that she was about to undertake, a low profile would be of the utmost importance and discretion.

Having drawn her Bentley to a slow halt in a side street well away from the curious eyes of passers-by, she approached a small newsagent's shop. Pressing the bell set in the well-worn wooden frame of the outside door, Anne wondered, a little apprehensively, as to what the outcome of her visit would be. 'What can I be doing for you?' Agatha's voice greeted her on opening the door. Anne hesitated. 'I hope you don't mind Mrs. Black, but I would like to have a word with you in private if it's not too inconvenient?' Agatha returned her gaze not bothering to disguise her surprise and anxious expression. 'Well I suppose you'd better come in then. Mind you it's not been my day for cleaning so you'll 'ave to excuse the mess.' 'Please don't worry' Anne tried to reassure her. 'I won't take up too much of your time,'

Agatha ushered Anne up the flight of stairs leading to the small dining room. 'I'll know you'll not be calling for a social visit.' Agatha began, 'I'll expect it will be something to do with your niece.' Anne felt a little uncertain and wished that her visit wasn't necessary. But there was no point fooling herself into a false complacency. It was necessary. 'Yes' she replied quietly. 'It is concerning Rebecca.' 'Well let's be hearing then' Agatha interrupted. 'As you are aware, Mrs. Black,' Anne continued 'Rebecca has been seeing your son Mark.' Agatha nodded. 'Well, I know this may sound harsh but I would like to see the relationship come to an end.' Agatha's face flushed a fiery red. 'Are you saying my son's not good enough for her? Is that what you've come to tell me?' a note of vehemence creeping into her voice. 'You and you're kind, you're all alike all with your noses in the air, in your big houses driving your fancy cars and your fancy ideas. And us folk, clean, honest living folk like we are, we're not good enough for you are we! We've no place with you, we don't belong do we?' Startled by Agatha's outburst, Anne rose from her chair. 'Please Mrs. Black it's nothing like that, nothing like that at all!' Agatha stared at Anne reproachfully. 'Well what is it then? Our Mark's a fine lad and he'll make some young lass a fine husband one day. He's a good head on his shoulders and he's as honest as the day is young! He doesn't want to marry your niece!' Anne looked surprised. 'Is that what he said?' she asked. 'That's what he's told me. He's not lied to me before, ever!' 'I still think their relationship should come to an end' Anne insisted. 'And how should I arrange that?' Agatha retorted. 'I can't tell my son what to do. Why don't you talk to Rebecca if that's the way you feel?' 'I can't do that either' Anne replied truthfully, 'she would never understand.' 'I don't understand either' Agatha replied sarcastically. The two women eyed each other in silence. 'Is your husband at home?' Anne asked, 'Perhaps it would be better if we all spoke about this together.' Agatha frowned. 'I don't want the likes of you upsetting my Tom. He won't be up until later this afternoon. Saturday is a busy day down in the shop.' 'What about Mark?' Anne asked. 'Will he be home soon?' 'No he won't. He's working too. Folks like us have to earn our money. We're not all born with silver spoons in our mouths.' Anne felt at a distinct disadvantage. There was no way she was going to rationalise with a woman like Mrs. Black. No way at all. She was so obviously deeply prejudiced that she hadn't even begun to let Anne explain her reasoning or fears. 'Can we wait and speak with your husband?' Anne asked apprehensively, 'I promise it won't upset him.' Agatha fumbled with the front of her pinafore. 'I don't know about that. I don't see why you have to be coming here in the first place.' 'Look' Anne pleaded, 'do you honestly feel in your heart it could possibly work. Mark's a very nice young man,

I know that, but Rebecca's been brought up in a totally different way. I don't want to sound snobbish. It isn't that at all, but surely you can see the divide between them is so very, very wide. Once the bloom of love begins to wear off, they'll have too many differences!' Agatha listened, deep down feeling the same way herself. How many times had she told Mark that Rebecca wasn't for him? And she had her own memories too with all those folk up on the hill. Why did they always have to have everything their own way? Tom's voice intruded into her thoughts. 'I've shut shop for a short while.' He nodded at Anne. 'I thought something must be wrong for you to be coming here!' 'It's Mark and Rebecca' Agatha could hardly get the words out of her mouth fast enough. 'She doesn't approve of our son seeing her, Tom.' Tom raised his eyebrows questioningly before sitting down slowly in his armchair at the same time fumbling with the paper for his cigarette. 'Make me a cup of tea, love. Maybe Miss Henderson would like one too?' Anne nodded. She was tired, nervous and frustrated. What was she doing here, she asked herself. Why hadn't she let things rest? But in her heart she knew she had no option but to come. For once she had to do what was right, but it was hard. There was no running away this time. If only Sam were here now. If only! A small diamond shaped tear rested in the corner of her eye refusing to trickle downwards on her cheek. She could feel Tom staring at her, his eyes her mind and thoughts. 'Don't fret now' he whispered, 'Don't be upsetting yourself. I understand you know. You'd be surprised how much I understand!' Anne slowly drank her tea. The atmosphere was less tense now that Tom had joined them. 'I'm sorry if I appear to have offended you in anyway' she began falteringly, 'but that wasn't the intention. It has been very difficult for me over the past few years and I am only doing what I believe to be right.' Agatha regarded Anne with a look of scepticism. 'I think' Anne continued, 'I have no option but to tell you something. Something which you may never understand but I hope you will forgive me for.' Anne hesitated as she replaced her cup and saucer with a trembling hand on the table next to her. Agatha and Tom watched her curiously. Anne looked up nervously trying to muster some strength before continuing. 'Rebecca is Sam's daughter. She is my child and your grand-daughter.'

Agatha stared at Anne in total disbelief her eyes wide with incredulity and amazement. 'Tom, what's she saying? Tom did you hear what she said?' Tom shook his head. 'Yes, I heard love. I heard!' He sat quietly, his head buried in his hands. 'I'm so dreadfully sorry' Anne stammered, wiping away the tears which were now slowly trickling down her cheeks. 'But you're her Aunt!' Agatha spluttered. 'She's your sister Sarah's child.' 'No!' Anne replied, surprised by the forcefulness of her own voice, 'No she is my daughter and the daughter of your son Sam.' Agatha winced. No-one had mentioned Sam's name for such a long while. Tears welled up in her eyes before cascading down her cheeks. Tom moved towards her and she buried her head on his shoulder and wept.

'There, there' he comforted. 'There now, let's hear what Miss Henderson has to say. Come on my girl, it's time to listen now.'

Anne slowly related how she had met Sam. 'I was deeply in love with Sam and he with me. But my parents would never accept him as a suitable husband. In the end we were meeting secretly until one day he received his call up papers. It was then we decided that once the war was over, we would marry despite all the disapprovals. The night before he left he gave me this ring which I have always worn.' She lifted her hand and fondled the thin gold band on the third finger of her right hand. 'To us we were man and wife in God's eyes, and that was all that mattered,' Anne paused, 'but he never came back and I was carrying his child. My parents knew of course but no matter how I pleaded with them they insisted the child would be taken from me at birth and given a new home. Sarah was pregnant too. We both went into labour at the same time. Her child was stillborn. That's when I pleaded with the mid wife to substitute my baby for hers, Sam's child.' Anne paused. She could see the midwife's face clearly as if it were yesterday. Your sister's broken water the midwife's voice spoke softly followed by the sadness. 'Sarah's baby was stillborn and my baby was yet to be born. My beautiful baby girl and only the midwife knew. She must have seen my heartache and how I wanted my baby to grow up near me. She understood and took our secret to her grave!'

Tom and Agatha sat in complete silence. 'Why didn't you come to us?' Agatha asked, her voice trembling with emotion. 'We'd have given you and the baby a good home. Oh why didn't you come?' 'I couldn't' Anne replied, wiping another tear from her moist cheek. 'Don't you understand, no-one knew. My parents never would have allowed it and the scandal it would have caused. Perhaps if Sarah's baby would have lived, I may have done. But her baby was stillborn and Rebecca could inherit all that was rightfully hers. At the time it seemed the only and best solution.' Anne paused 'I think Sam would have thought so too.' Tom nodded. So much had happened in such a short time. He thought back to the afternoon when Rebecca had visited them. How she had reminded him of someone. Someone he hadn't seen for too long a while. He remembered how startled he was when he realised it was Sam's frank eyes he was looking into and Sam's same mannerisms. How his heart had pounded with the thoughts racing through his mind, trying to understand something that he could not fully comprehend. Nothing made sense. Then he'd been taken poorly, brought on by the fretting in his mind but it had all been true. Rebecca was Sam's daughter; his and Agatha's grandchild.

Anne sat motionless waiting for Agatha and Tom to speak. 'You must understand' she added falteringly, 'Rebecca must not hear the truth. Not yet anyway. Please understand that.' Tom and Agatha stared at Anne. There were so many questions but they would have to wait. They needed time to come to terms with what they had heard. And Mark! Their son Mark was Rebecca's uncle. Mark's brother was Rebecca's Father.

There was no possibility that they could, or should, continue seeing one another. Not now but that was another obstacle to be dealt with later. Now was the time for grieving and rejoicing. Now was the moment for all those tears to be shed to fill a river, a river that up until now had run dry.

Chapter 27

CHARLES MATTHEWS LISTENED intently as Anne related the events of the afternoon. 'Good Lord Anne' he inhaled deeply on his Davidoff cigar before continuing, 'Good Lord Anne why didn't you tell me what was going on! Why didn't you mention that Mark was who he is?' Anne wiped her eyes which were now bloodshot and tired. 'Charles, I had no idea who he was until Rebecca brought him home. As soon as I set eyes on him it was like seeing a ghost from the past. I knew he had to be related and it was only on visiting the Blacks that I discovered the truth. I didn't plan what happened only to voice the objections about Mark seeing Rebecca. It just came out and this time Charles, I couldn't face another lie!' Charles sat quietly for a moment his eyes far away in deep thought. 'How did the Blacks react?' he asked quietly. 'They were very upset as you can well imagine. They need time now to digest the enormity of what they have learned, time to adjust. Then we will meet up again.' 'What did they say about Rebecca and Mark?' Charles continued with his questioning.

'Nothing' Anne regarded Charles apologetically. 'It's a forgone fact that the two have to cease their relationship but at the moment we haven't gone into what the best solution is. Charles, please give me your advice. I need desperately to decide what the best way forward should be.' Charles grunted, 'It's a bit late for that Anne now that the horse has bolted so to speak. I am really now of the opinion that Rebecca has to be told everything no matter how painful it is going to be.' 'No!' Anne exclaimed. 'No Charles. Not yet. I cannot believe all this is happening and to think' she faltered, 'to think that my only fear was that Robert would prey on her for her money. That seems such a triviality now compared to this.' Charles nodded. 'In some ways I tend to agree with you. It certainly was the easier option to handle. Now it appears we have both.' Charles took another puff of his cigar. 'When will Rebecca be coming home?' 'On Monday' Anne replied. 'Robert apparently wanted to discuss his forthcoming plans to marry Lady Cynthia Cope. It's all very much of a hush hush. He asked her to visit to discuss his plans. In a way I was quite happy at the news in as much as Lady Cope is very wealthy in her own right.' 'Yes, I take your point' Charles agreed 'but you've certainly stirred up a hornet's nest with all these latest developments. Once again Anne, I do think you have no option but to tell Rebecca everything.' Anne shuddered again. 'God give me strength' she muttered under her breath. 'I'm certainly going to need it!'

Chapter 28

MOLLY BROUGHT ANNE her Sunday breakfast in bed. 'It's a beautiful day' she commented chirpily. 'I'll be off now if you're sure there's nothing you'll be requiring me to do.' 'Thank you Molly. Everything's fine. I shall be lunching with the Jacksons and a round of bridge is just what I'll be enjoying later.'

Molly checked the kitchen her thoughts elsewhere. Inwardly she felt disturbed at the way everything had been happening of late. Something wasn't right and the look of Miss Henderson this morning with her swollen eyes and tired face troubled her deeply. She was tempted to ask what was wrong and if there was anything she could do. But that wouldn't be right either. Then there was that lad Miss Rebecca brought home; the Blacks' son of all people. Not the nice gentry that normally came to call. 'He had no place here' she tutted to herself deep in thought as she went about her chores. 'It's an ill wind that blows no-one no good' she spoke out loud. 'Wait and see if I'll not be right!'

The black and white photograph in her morning newspaper stared back at Anne over her pot of Earl Grey Tea. She read its caption slowly, taking in every word of its deliberate sarcastic diatribe. 'Robert Lawson and ladies enjoying yet another night out on the tiles! Will this casanova ever settle down to another period of matrimonial bliss? Accompanied by his once estranged daughter, Rebecca and Lady Cynthia Cope were seen leaving The Clarice in the early hours of Sunday morning! Perhaps this intriguing intimate picture bodes well for more intriguing news to come. Watch this space!'

A look of horror crossed Anne's face. Now that Rebecca had been identified in the media as Robert's daughter there was positively no way that an ounce of scandal could be exposed. Anne could see the headlines screaming out in their latest copy 'Robert Lawson in daughter tragedy. The secret of the daughter that never was. A story full of lies, intrigue and deception!'

Anne fumbled with the small gold diamond encrusted pill box which she always kept on her bedside table. Her fingers trembling she retrieved two small white insignificant tablets which she washed down with some freshly squeezed orange juice. Resting her head on the plumped up pillows behind her, she wished deep down there was a way to leave all the confusion behind; longed for a way to be rid of her guilt and to be free from all the torment and pain.

Rebecca stared at her Aunt, anger and hatred contorting her once placid features into those of a demented being. 'How could you do this to me?' she snarled. 'How could you put me through so much hell, torment and embarrassment?' Anne watched her unable to offer any words of comfort or solace. 'I'm sorry Rebecca, I truly am sorry!' 'Sorry!' Rebecca spat the words back at her. 'You've wrecked my life, my future, my past and all you can say is your sorry!' She laughed, a low guttural laugh spiked with increasing hysteria. 'You're evil Aunt Anne, evil. How could you have done such a thing! You substituted me for a dead child, your sister's child. You let her bring me up as her own while you looked on and my Father? How do you think he will feel?' 'Your Father is dead' Anne scoffed. 'The man you call your Father never cared about you, never bothered with you or you're so called Mother. Your so called Father cared only for one thing. Money! He wasn't bothered if you lived or died so don't dare to speak to me about your Father!' 'Oh yes' Rebecca taunted, 'oh yes but we mustn't forget that he isn't my Father. I am a bastard born out of wedlock sired by the village idiot!' 'Rebecca how can you speak like this; how can you say such things!' 'But I can' Rebecca's voice mocked, 'I hate you! You're vile, loathsome and mean nothing to me. Nothing! I may have come from your womb but you're not and never will be my Mother. You disgust me.' Anne felt the tears stinging her eyes. 'Rebecca, let me explain. Let me tell you how I felt and my feelings. Please give me that one chance. Please!' Anne froze at the look of hatred written across Rebecca's face. 'I don't want to listen to you or ever have to see you again!'

Anne caught a glimpse of the small dagger and felt the sharp point of cold sharp steel as it made its first piercing incision into her pale sparsely covered flesh. Wet, sticky drops of blood trickled slowly down her warm skin. A feeling of nausea engulfed her whole being and her body felt wet and heavy with exhaustion. 'Rebecca' Anne gasped, 'Rebecca please forgive me. I'm so very sorry.' Rebecca stared down coldly at her Aunt oblivious to the blood and pain. 'It's too late to be sorry. This way no-one need ever know. It's much too late Aunt Anne. Rest in Peace. It's all over now!' Her high pitched laugh echoed throughout the room. 'Yes Aunt Anne it's definitely all over now.

Anne forced her lids to open. Her head felt heavy as if held down by an iron weight. She peered nervously at the blue lace bodice of her nightdress. It was soaked through. The bone china teacup, from which she had been drinking, lay on its side across her bosom which was now sodden with cold Earl Grey tea. Reaching for a paper tissue she attempted to dry herself before leaving the bed and made her way to the bathroom the reality of the nightmare still haunting her thoughts.

Chapter 29

TOM BLACK SAT in his armchair puffing on yet another cigarette. 'Don't you think you should give yourself a rest?' Agatha reproached him. 'Yes love, you're right but you know how it is!' Agatha nodded. She was finding it difficult to absorb everything Anne had told them but somehow all the tears had released something deep down inside that had been waiting to pour forth. But Tom, he was different. For once he had been the one to fret and brood. For once she was the strong one, the one with vast amounts of inner strength and reserve to cope with the situation.

'We've a grand-daughter!' she exclaimed proudly, 'A beautiful grand-daughter. A wonderful gift from Sam' Tom grunted. 'What's the matter Tom?' she asked hesitantly. 'What's the matter?' he snapped back angrily. 'How can you be asking what's the matter!' Agatha felt her body tense at his terse remark. 'Our son's totally besotted with a young lass who's his brother's child and you ask what the matter is?' Agatha shook her head. 'I know' she mumbled apologetically, 'but at the same time I can't help rejoicing we have a beautiful grand-daughter. I can't help that Tom. Mark will understand. He's a good head on his shoulders and he's young and strong. We'll have to tell him gently. He'll soon get over it and he has got Wendy. He also told me he is fond of Rebecca in a platonic sort of way so there won't be any headache!' 'I doubt you're right' Tom shook his head in disbelief. Your son won't be telling you all. I doubt your right!'

Agatha was busying herself in the kitchen when it happened. She heard Tom cry out in pain and his ashen face told her everything she needed to know. 'Your Dad's taken poorly. You'd better come quickly!' A neighbour broke the news to Mark.

Mark comforted his Mother, enfolding her in his strong caring arms. 'How is he Ma?' he asked fearing her reply. 'They say he's stable son. We just have to wait.' 'How about a sweet cup of tea Ma it will help.' They both sat in silence fearing the worse, too frightened and worried to speak. 'He just came over bad' Agatha whispered, 'and so white too.' 'There, there' Mark consoled her. 'He's tough is Dad. He'll be all right.' 'Mr. Mark Black?' The gentle voice of the nurse interrupted. Mark stood up rigidly as if to attention. 'Please come this way' the nurse motioned towards the double swing doors leading into a narrow corridor. 'What about Ma?' Mark questioned. 'Please come' she insisted gently. 'Your Mother's already been sitting with your Father for a while. Its better she has a rest!'

Agatha waited anxiously for Mark to return. 'Dad wants to see you Ma' he told her a little while later. Agatha noticed how pale Mark was looking now and the troubled look written across his face. 'Don't worry Ma, he's a good fighter. He won't give up that easy!'

Chapter 30

ANNE HEAVED A sigh at the sound of Rebecca's return. The long weekend had seemed like an eternity and events were taking over at a very rapid pace. No more the tranquillity which once bathed her with its very presence. No more the serenity and peacefulness of so many days long past. Now there was conflict and turmoil, guilt and unease. Now was the beginning. Everything else was dead; ashes in an empty hearth, cold, dark and uninviting. Shakespeare's words kept racing around in her mind. 'Now is the winter of our discontent.'

'I've something to tell you' she told Rebecca as they sat quietly over a strong cup of tea. 'Mark called. His Father's suffered another heart attack. He's so dreadfully sorry but he says he can't see you.' Rebecca could not hide her puzzled and hurt expression. 'What do you mean, he can't see me? Honestly Aunt Anne I can't believe he would say that!' Anne returned her questioning gaze. 'I'm only telling you what he asked me to' she added gently. 'I expect he's terribly worried and doesn't want to burden you.' 'But this is so unlike him!' Rebecca replied. 'Surely he would want me to make contact!'

Rebecca showered hastily before changing into a plain dark brown skirt and cream silk blouse. She was terribly confused at Mark's message and knew her Aunt would only have told her the truth. How could he shut her out at a time like this when she should be there to offer comfort and support? No, this was a mistake made unintentionally in a moment of distress. He obviously did not want to burden or worry her.

The sign on the front of the newsagent's door read 'closed' as Rebecca drew her mini to a halt outside. She pressed the bell anxiously awaiting the sound of some movement from within. Mark's white drawn face stared at her through the partially open door. 'You'd better come in' he motioned, opening the door wider. 'I'm so sorry Mark' Rebecca whispered slowly climbing the narrow stairs to the small dining room. 'How is your Father now?' Mark shrugged his shoulders. 'He's a fighter but this time it's more serious than the last. This time they don't know. Ma's at the hospital now. She doesn't want to leave his side.' 'Aunt Anne gave me your message. Why did you say you didn't want to see me?' A tinge of colour touched Mark's cheeks. 'I'm sorry Rebecca. So much has happened and I don't know what will be happening. I just think its best that we don't see one another for a while. Ma needs me now and if Dad pulls through I want to be helping him too. I just can't think about myself.' Rebecca felt the tears welling up inside. 'But what about me Mark? What about us? I thought you loved me!' Mark looked at her sheepishly. 'Rebecca love doesn't come into it at all any more. It's all for the best believe me.' 'But I want to see your Father' she stammered, 'will you let me do that?' 'Of course' Mark replied, trying to ignore the knots which felt so tight in the pit of his stomach. 'He would dearly love that!'

Rebecca waited for Mark as he locked up before leaving. He sat next to her deep in thought as she drove towards the hospital. 'Mark, please don't upset yourself. Don't worry about me. You must do what you have to do but please remember I am here for you.' 'Yes, I know that Rebecca. Thank you'.

Rebecca sat quietly at Tom's bedside, watching him labouring for each and every breath. 'Tom its Rebecca' she whispered gently enfolding his frail hand in hers, 'Tom, its Rebecca, Mark's friend. Do you remember me?' Tom's eyes opened slowly and for a fleeting moment, a smile surfaced across his face softening his pale features in warmth. His grand-daughter, Sam's daughter was with him and he was going to be all right. He was at peace with the world now. He would tell Sam all about her and how beautiful she was. How she had the same eyes and mannerisms. How she was so much like her dad. 'Sam you should be proud of yourself son. You have a beautiful daughter. You would be so proud. I just want you to know that. Your Ma and I are so happy. Your daughter's safe and we love her son as much as we love you.'

Chapter 31

MARK WATCHED HIS Mother apprehensively. She hadn't come to terms with his Father's death as yet and why should she have? He hadn't but he had to be firm as there was nothing to be gained from falling apart. Doctor Jones had prescribed some medication but all it seemed to achieve was to make her sleepy. All she did in fact was sleep and once awake was, as he described it to the doctor later, a walking zombie. 'Give her time' he was assured, 'it takes time to grieve and to face the loss of a loved one.' Mark didn't object to that. 'But how can she grieve when she's so full of pills?' Doctor Jones nodded his head sympathetically. 'It will pass Mark, believe me. Has she spoken to Reverend Norris? A sense of belonging with the church may help her spiritually and renew some of the faith in living.' 'I'll try to do something' Mark added at the same time not too hopeful of achieving any more results.

Agatha's unkempt hair and ashen face did nothing to dispel Mark's feelings of hopelessness on arriving back at the shop later that day. 'Ma' he chided, 'why don't you change into something fresh and make yourself look a little better.' 'What for?' Agatha sighed, 'what for?' 'For Dad, Ma, for Dad.' 'He's dead son' she stifled a sob, 'he's dead and I blame those folks on the Hill. Those posh stuck up people, that's who!' 'Ma, how can you say that. How can you possibly think that way? I thought you liked Rebecca.' Agatha continued oblivious to his words. 'I told you she was not for you. How many times did I tell you that? But would you listen to me? No! And even your Pa was put under her spell. Those folks are evil. Evil as can be. If they'd stayed out of our life Tom would still be alive now. Still be alive to breathe in the air around us, to be with me where he belongs. I tell you I loathe them and her!' 'Who Ma?' Mark asked hesitatingly. 'That Anne woman, that's who! The woman who says she is Rebecca's Mother. And I don't believe any more all her stories and carrying on that she bore Rebecca or that she is Sam's child. She's an evil woman is that one and our Sam would never have entertained the likes of her!' Mark listened but the words meant nothing to him. His Mother was pushing away everything she didn't want or couldn't understand. All this, all this and Pa's dead, he thought sadly. Deep down he felt perhaps his Mother was right. Not in all circumstances, but he had to admit to the fact that his Father looked strained after meeting Rebecca. As if, as if his whole insides were being torn apart. Like too many memories, too much sadness, that he couldn't possibly cope with all at once. 'Yes, he was in poor health and it's my fault' Mark reproached himself. 'If only I'd never met Rebecca. If only we had not continued to see one another. So many ifs, so many.......' He stopped himself there. What was happening to him now! Surely his Mother's depressive feelings weren't dragging him down too. 'Pull yourself together Mark Black' he told himself. 'How can you help Ma if you too start thinking this way . I'll make you a nice cup of tea Ma' he said encouragingly. 'It'll make you feel better and put some colour in your cheeks.' Agatha stared at him with a vacant expression of incomprehension. 'Ma, did you hear me? Did you hear what I just said?' Agatha just stared. 'I'd rather be dead' she muttered. 'I'd rather they put me in the coffin with your Pa. Without him there's nothing, nothing. Let me die, the sooner the better.' Mark looked on despairingly. His world had been turned upside down and now this. He loved Rebecca and he was missing her desperately. He needed her, longed for her so very much. Often at night he would feel a tightening in his groin, a surging so strong, that he battled with himself to let go. He could still touch her beautiful auburn hair and see those frank hazel eyes and soft lips. Sweet luscious lips and he longed to kiss them. How he longed for her touch, her smell, her silky soft skin. Never had he felt this way before and he knew deep, deep down, he would never feel this way again. He sensed a burning behind his eyes. 'Grown men don't cry' he heard his Father saying on his death bed. 'Grown men are forceful, strong and here he was acting like a baby. 'Oh Lord, Oh Lord, he moaned, when is this going to end! Tell me Lord, when?'

Chapter 32

MORE THAN A month had passed since the funeral. Summer had turned to autumn and the chill of the winter months ahead could be felt as the darker evenings drew in closer and closer.

'I'm really looking forward to Father's wedding. Won't you please accept the invitation to come too?' Anne looked at Rebecca's pale face which had now become alive with the anticipation at the forthcoming event. It was good to see her finally showing an interest in something again after all this time instead of brooding and moping around. Since the death of Tom Black, Rebecca had stopped seeing Mark and Anne had not asked why. It was better that way she reflected. As for Tom and Agatha, she presumed they had thought it best not to tell Mark either. She pondered on Tom's death, how sad it had happened and how sorry she was. She had carefully selected the flowers for a wreath and had written to Agatha expressing hers and Rebecca's sincere condolences. More than that would have been an intrusion. Everything had worked out for the best in the end, she thought guiltily.

'No Rebecca, I have decided not to accept your Father's invitation to his wedding. Believe me Rebecca he only asked me out of politeness and respect for you.' 'Oh you are silly' Rebecca admonished, 'perhaps you will change your mind.' 'No Rebecca. Not this time. Just enjoy yourself to the full and you can tell us all about it when you come back.'

David was so happy to see Rebecca again. 'It's been a long time' he scolded. 'Don't be silly David. It's not even two months. That isn't long!' David grinned. 'Have it your way' he groaned. 'Your Mother looks wonderful' Rebecca sighed. 'Your Father thinks so too! Just look at his face. You'd think it was their first marriage the way they are carrying on.'

Rebecca watched in admiration as Lady Cynthia mingled with her guests her pale ivory satin suit complemented with dusky pink pearl buttons and touches of pure cream lace emphasised the beauty of her pale flawless English complexion. She looked wonderful, and her Father in his grey morning suit with tails and matching top hat, was a picture of elegance and so very handsome too. 'Come on Rebecca it's time for some champers now don't you think!' David gently touched her arm. Rebecca startled. 'I'm so sorry I was miles away' she apologised. 'They look so very, very happy.' Mark's face was still in her mind haunting her thoughts. How he had ended their relationship and how she missed him so dreadfully. Her stomach felt tight, nervous tight knots playing havoc with her usual feelings of well-being. She knew what was happening to her. She didn't need a doctor to explain. But Mark didn't want her and she was not going to use this as an excuse for him to acknowledge her existence once more.

'Well Rebecca' David urged, 'let's eat then we can talk about what you've been up to since you returned to Roynick.' 'Rebecca' Cynthia called. As she looked up to reply a beautiful bouquet of pink and cream roses intermingled with sprays of freebase gently drifted towards her. She blushed as the guests applauded their acceptance in her waiting outstretched arms. 'You are next!' her Father winked, a broad grin covering his face from ear to ear.

So much had happened since her last visit to London. How could she have been so stupid to think that Mark would have married her and how stupid to think that he wouldn't have felt cheated as the provider and carer in their life. He would only be happy with a girl of his own means, a girl who would depend on him in every sense of the word. There were far less of his types than gigolos she thought ruefully. So many men would seize the opportunity to feed off a woman's wealth, ready to bleed them dry. She closed her eyes fighting the emotions which were playing havoc with her very existence.

'I want you Mark' She had whispered, 'I want you so very, very much!' He had been a gentle lover, so kind and caring. Everything was going to be all right . Nothing was going to stop them from being together.'

His hands had caressed every part of her exploring the sensitivity of her warm, silky skin and the fullness of her beautifully proportioned breasts. She had tingled with excitement at his touch, so wonderfully sensuous and caring and tasted his lips, responsive, sweet and his mouth, a velvety cavern that her tongue explored longingly and lovingly. His touch, his all, how could she possibly forget the longing he aroused in her, the stirring and aching between her thighs, and when he entered her most sacred part, the feeling of oneness, total togetherness, a different world! His body, so amazingly masculine that she could only look at with awe and one which she alone would love and cherish. He was all she could possibly want and she was ecstatically happy.

'Another champers' David coaxed. 'We've really got so much to celebrate today!' Rebecca smiled. 'Yes but only half a glass' Rebecca responded. 'I'm beginning to feel the effects now and I can't say I am used to drinking so much at this time of day!' 'How about we amble back to my place and relax there?' David suggested. 'OK by me' Rebecca replied, anxious now to disappear and unwind. It had been a wonderful day and she felt completely relaxed as David made his way through the late afternoon traffic. They approached his mews house which was tucked away in an old fashioned cobbled side street off the Bayswater Road within walking distance from Hyde Park. She was pleasantly surprised to find that even though David led a bachelor's existence, his home still had that indefinable woman's touch. Two golden Labradors bounded around in excitement on their return, eager to enter the house from the small back garden. 'You do like dogs?' he asked. 'Of course' Rebecca replied. 'How could I possibly not?'

They had indulged in more champagne until, without any feelings of awkwardness they had both surrendered to tiredness.

Chapter 33

'GOD I FEEL awful' Rebecca groaned. David propped his head on his elbow and looked down into her heavy lashed hazel eyes. 'I love you' he whispered, 'from the first day I set eyes on you.' His hand caressed her naked body, gently outlining the small roundness of her firm breasts, continuing downwards over her taut belly and beyond. 'I love you' he whispered hoarsely drawing her close to him, wanting her so much that his whole body tensed with longing and the pain of anticipation. She was the most exquisite creature he had hardly dared to imagine. 'What's wrong?' he asked tentatively, sensing a sadness he could not explain. 'Nothing David' she lied. 'I was just far away and thinking how strange life is.' 'And wonderful too,' David murmured, pulling her so close to him until nothing could possibly prise them apart.

Anne could hardly believe her ears. 'You've what!' she exclaimed on hearing Rebecca's words. 'I'm going to marry David' she repeated. 'But you hardly know him and it's so quick!' 'Does that matter? I really know so much even in such a short time.' Anne hesitated. It was too soon after Mark, too soon in any event and something was wrong. 'Is there anything you want to tell me' she probed hesitantly. 'No' Rebecca replied. 'There's nothing to tell only that I won't be leaving you completely. We'll spend weekends here and sometimes I'll stay longer. I would like to have our wedding reception in London. Do you mind?' 'Of course not Rebecca, but when can I meet David?' 'Next weekend, he's driving down and I know you'll adore him'

'My goodness Charles' Anne looked thoughtful. 'Can you imagine all this happening in such a short space of time?' Charles stared into space, 'No my dear, not really. And to think of all the unnecessary worry you put yourself through!' Anne nodded. 'Yes Charles, you are right. Perhaps I should have never made that visit to the Blacks. What they never knew wouldn't have made any difference as things turned out.' Anne hesitated. 'I'm sorry Charles, that wasn't a very Christian thought. Do forgive me.' Charles smiled, 'Don't be silly Anne. I tend to agree with you, but that's all in the past. What's this David chap like? It must be very exciting for you!' Anne shook her head, 'He sounds very nice. Rebecca will be bringing him home next weekend. All I really know is he a Veterinary Surgeon and has been married before but his wife wasn't compatible with his work or with him. I am really looking forward to meeting him and I hope you can join us for dinner whilst he is here.' 'Yes, of course. I wouldn't miss it for the world. Thank you Anne.'

Chapter 34

ANNE WATCHED DAVID carefully. His whole demeanour was one of utmost self-confidence. Every move, every nuance, she noted with the eye of a Mother about to entrust her daughter to the care and love of another being.

Charles, David and Rebecca were now relaxing in Anne's sitting room chatting animatedly over coffee and liqueurs. Charles slowly inhaled on his Davidoff cigar, savouring its taste and aroma. He approved of David, a fine mature man he thought to himself. Anne felt very content too, surprised how well everything had progressed so far and completely at ease with the situation. She had been more than happy on meeting David to find that he was very mature and charming. Someone Rebecca would be able to rely on and relate to. He was taller than Rebecca by at least 4 inches and his features were angular and rugged. A shot of jet black hair, which fell in a slight quiff onto his forehead gave him a slightly boyish appearance.

David leaned over towards Rebecca who was sitting close by on the three piece chintz settee, gently placing her hand in his. 'I hope you approve of my taking charge of your niece' he smiled at Anne, his dark brown eyes twinkling in amusement. Anne responded with a smile. 'As long as you cherish her no matter what, how could I possibly have any objections?' 'Rebecca mentioned' David continued on a more serious note 'you were happy with our plans for a champagne and strawberry reception after the wedding nuptials have been taken care of at the Registry Office.' Anne winced. 'I always imagined Rebecca as a beautiful bride walking down the aisle in Church but if that is what you want!' Rebecca squeezed David's hand affectionately, encouragingly. 'Yes Aunt Anne, it is really what we both want and there would be delays and complications with a Church wedding now that David's divorced.' 'Of course my dear. How stupid of me to have forgotten that. Please forgive me.'

Anne noticed the flush highlighting Rebecca's cheeks. All the excitement and preparation was beginning to take its toll on her niece and the last thing she wanted was for Rebecca to work herself into a state of anxiety. Her thoughts wandered back to her meeting with Mark and how happy and relaxed Rebecca had been then. Now she seemed strained, worried perhaps, but was it any wonder with everything progressing so quickly and all out of the blue. 'Yes, yes, the Savoy it is and I insist on paying for the function whether you object or not.' 'Oh Aunt Anne' Rebecca's filled over with emotion, 'we don't want you to pay for the wedding. All we want is to have you near and dear to us!' Anne shook her head in disapproval. 'I've never heard of such nonsense so there is nothing, absolutely nothing to discuss. I'm really looking forward to it and my stay at the Savoy!' 'Me too,' Charles added, 'me too!'

Molly bubbled over with excitement. 'What do you think Arthur' she chuckled, 'our Rebecca's found herself a proper gentleman and we'll be going to London for the wedding'. 'Bit quick weren't it?' Arthur mumbled. 'What about that Black boy? What became of him?' Molly slowly wiped her hands on the red chequered teacloth. 'I expect she came to her senses, what with old Tom passing on and all that. So unexpected and so sad. Yes, I expect that's what it was. Lord knows what I'm going to wear with all these folk from London being there an'all. Lord knows what I'm going to wear!'

Chapter 35

'DAVID,' REBECCA'S VOICE trembled slightly, 'David I've something I have to tell you.' David turned onto his side facing Rebecca. The faint light of the moon which peered in through the half drawn curtains of the bedroom, accentuated the earnestness of Rebecca's pale face. 'What is it?' David murmured his fingers caressing her rich auburn hair. 'David, I'm pregnant!' The words tumbled out. David sat bolt upright, his face registering complete surprise. 'You're what!' he gasped incredulously. 'I'm pregnant' Rebecca repeated. 'But how?' David stammered. 'I thought you were taking a precaution!' 'I was, I mean I did. But with all the excitement, I just, well, forgot!' David frowned. 'Have you seen a doctor?' 'No, but I know I'm pregnant David. I can't explain, but I just know.' David sat quietly for a while, deep in thought absorbing what Rebecca had sprung on him so suddenly out of the blue. 'Come here' he murmured, drawing her closely to him. 'Is it all right?' Rebecca asked nervously, 'are you angry?' 'Of course I'm not' he lied. He had so wanted Rebecca all to himself. Wanted to spend so much time with her alone enjoying her presence and so many new intimacies and now there was a child between them. An intruder! It was much too soon and he was angry and upset. But it was his child and his seed of his being. How selfishly he was behaving. How could he possibly think like this? Drawing Rebecca closer to him he held her tightly against his flesh feeling a deep hunger of longing. 'Rebecca darling, I love you so very, very much. Of course I'm not angry, a little selfish perhaps. I want you all to myself and don't want to share you with anyone. But it's our child and that's all that matters and we must make the most of the time that we have alone before the baby arrives. I do love you!' Rebecca felt her stomach tighten at his words. She closed her eyes, desperately fighting back the tears. 'I'm sorry' she whispered, her head buried in his shoulder. 'I'm so dreadfully sorry!' And it was Mark's arms holding her so tightly once more, Mark's face and Mark's baby. 'I'm so sorry' she whispered quietly before finally drifting off to sleep.

Chapter 36

SHE HAD INSISTED that Mark meet her a week prior to her wedding. They had met at Copse Corner and sat huddled together in her blue mini as they talked.

'Mark, I'm expecting your child' she had told him in a cool, clear, dispassionate voice so detached from the churning anguish and turmoil which she was feeling inside. His mouth fell open in amazement and his eyes glazed over in horror. 'You what?' he spluttered, unable to take in the enormity of her words. 'I wasn't going to tell you Mark. You decided you didn't want me even though I loved you. I'm marrying someone who loves me and who will love my child as his own.' 'You've told him about me then and the baby?' 'No Mark, I haven't. He believes he is the Father of our child and that's the way it will always be. But I did want you to know that I am having your baby. That is so important to me Mark, but I didn't want you to marry me just because I was carrying your child.' Mark's face had turned a ghostly white. 'Oh Rebecca' he cried, tears streaming down his cheeks. 'I do love you. You'll never

ever know how much but I can't marry you and you can't have the baby!' He tried to stem the flow of tears while Rebecca held him gently in her arms not understanding these words and the unleashing of so many emotions. 'Rebecca there's something I have to tell you. Oh God forgive me, I just don't know whether I should or not!' Rebecca stared at him, trying to make sense of what was happening.

'The night my Father died' Mark continued, 'he called me to his bedside. He told me about my brother Sam and how he had loved a young girl and how they used to meet in secret because her family would never have approved of their being together. He also told me how my brother was called up for the war and how he died.' Mark paused and drew Rebecca into his arms, aching with love and tenderness. 'I love you Rebecca more than anything in this world but I can't marry you!' Tears streamed down his face once more as she caressed him fondling his hair and face. 'The young girl had become pregnant by my brother and eventually gave birth to a baby girl.' Rebecca watched Mark anxiously. 'Mark, what's all this got to do with me? None of this makes any sense.' Mark paused, sucking on his breath unsure as to what he should do or say next. 'Rebecca, the baby girl was you and the young girl was your Aunt Anne!' Rebecca sat rigidly in shock trying to absorb what Mark had said. 'What on earth are you talking about? What are you saying for heaven's sake? I've heard of some stories but your Father certainly had a field day telling this fairy-tale on his death bed. He was obviously delirious and you believed it all! Oh Mark, how could you!' 'Rebecca it's true. Believe me it's the honest truth. Your Mother Sarah had a stillborn child and your Aunt begged the midwife to substitute you in her place so she wouldn't lose you. So you could be brought up in the House on the Hill and inherit everything in the years to come. That way she could watch you grow and she could be near you always'. Rebecca sat silently staring in front of her gripping Mark's arm. She was trembling with shock at what Mark had said. A nightmare was unfolding before her and yet she could not accept any of what she was hearing. It was too much to absorb, too much to accept and too much to come to terms with. The old man, Mark's Father, delirious on his death bed, of that she had not the slightest doubt. Why he should have made up such a stupid, grotesque tale, she had no idea. And poor Mark, he was obviously taken in by this ludicrous and outrageous story for whatever reasons, in his subconscious mind. The enormity of the outcome of his words gradually dawned on her. No wonder he had finished their relationship and refused to see or have anything to do with her. Mark really believed his brother was her Father! That was preposterous. 'Mark darling, I can't convince you this is all a lie, a fairy-tale, because it's what you want to believe. If this is what you have to believe, I can't change that either. We could go and talk to Aunt Anne and I know she would tell you also that your Father was in no state of mind in his last hours. But if that's what you have to believe, I can think of no other way to convince you it is wrong. I will have your child and I know you will understand why. That will be our secret. A secret we will keep between us for however many years to come!'

Chapter 37

REBECCA STARED AT the pale face reflected in the dressing table mirror, eyes vacant, and cheeks pallid and wan. 'Pregnancy is supposedly a beautiful transition' she thought sadly, her mind in a whirl. She was not in love with David, in fact, she analysed coldly she was using him. Yes, he was kind, attentive and adoring, but none the less she was not in love with him, and Mark? Mark had rejected her choosing to listen to the ranting and raving of a man sucking in his last breath before death. Death, the all infinite, the all-encompassing, the finality of one's conscious being! Rebecca felt a cold ripple surface over her body; and then what of the hereafter? What then? A sea of nonentity for evermore, Amen!

Depressed and dejected, Rebecca gazed at her reflection once more. 'How can I eject this life within me?' she brooded. 'It belongs to us both, Mark and I. How can I terminate a living, breathing foetus?' Confused by her thoughts and her feelings of despondency tears flowed down her cheeks, rivulets of tears that solved nothing, only a reminder of her surfacing grief and anguish.

'Only one more week to the wedding' Anne sighed. The fitter looked across at Anne, a broad smile covering her face. Rebecca stood quietly as she rummaged around for some pins. 'I don't know Rebecca, but for a bride to be you should be as thin as a rake and here I am, having to let out the seams, not take them in!' Rebecca tossed her head back in a semi-defiant gesture. 'Really Mrs. Glenby I'm not going to starve myself to death due to pre-nuptial nerves. I've always been a practical person, haven't I Aunt Anne?' Anne nodded. 'Nevertheless' Anne added jokingly, 'I'm going to ask Molly to cut down on some of the rich food you seem to be indulging in of late. We really can't have Mrs. Glenby making alterations the actual day of your wedding!' Mrs. Glenby chuckled, a deep infectious chuckle which had the effect of encompassing anyone near enough to hear. 'Well that's all I have to do now' she added thoughtfully, checking the floor for any pins which may have gone astray. 'The florist has a swatch of the material' she added. 'No doubt your Father will be so excited at the thought of giving you away!' Anne turned her head to one side not wishing Rebecca to see the look of contempt which was now only too visible. 'He's giving her away' she thought, 'but he's never bothered to see her in the past. The fact that she is not his true daughter is neither here nor there' she muttered under her breath. 'Did you ask me something' Rebecca asked.

'No Rebecca, just talking to myself. The first signs of old age I should imagine.'

Alone, Rebecca hesitantly fingered the pure guipure lace of her bridal dress. It was so beautiful. 'Pure lace for a pure bride' she reflected. 'But the bride is pregnant and with another man's child.' Not quite the scenario she had anticipated for herself at such an important time in her life. But was it important? As far as she was concerned, No! David. Dear David, so kind, so true, but not the man she wanted to marry. She could feel the tears stinging her eyes, tears so many of late. Tears she never knew existed, tears she could not control and tears that served no purpose, only to puff her eyes and make her appear more tired than she really was. And the baby, she wondered at the marvel, the wondrous feat of nature which was growing inside her, day by day, hour by hour, and minute by minute. She marvelled at her body and tried to visualise the natural shape it would follow throughout the coming months. She sensed David's fingers softly outlining the shape of her belly as if eager to see the transformation which would slowly and deliberately take place. But where were Mark's hands, his gentle sensitive touch which aroused her so much with the promise of eroticism and love. 'What am I going to do? What am I going to do?' she asked, the question falling into an empty vacuum of space.

Chapter 38

ROBERT LAWSON RELAXED over a dry Martini. The afternoon sunlight provided a hazy glow as it manoeuvred its way in and out of the open spaces behind the silk blind in Lady Cynthia Cope's drawing room. He had spent the main part of the afternoon relaxing and discussing plans for Rebecca's wedding day. The arrangements had been taken care of by Anne for the reception at the Savoy and the guest list on his side had been executed expediently due to such short notice. His guest list, he pondered, had not been too long, on the contrary. He had not invited many of his socialite friends. Cynthia's family, of course, made up a substantial amount and a few others. He was feeling quite contented now, surprisingly so, in fact, having given up his bachelor apartment and now ensconced in the affluent surroundings of Cadogan Square.

Their honeymoon had been a wedding surprise from Cynthia and how wonderful it had been too! They had flown from London to Aruba where they had spent a couple of days relaxing on the white sandy beaches of the hotel's private island and by night, had dined in quaint restaurants of their own choosing. Casinos were located at practically every vantage point and his winning streak was providing free flowing dollars which they spent in the many exclusive duty free shops. After a couple of days, they had joined a cruise liner visiting many of the Caribbean islands dotted along the way. On returning to Aruba, they had flown to Miami to relax and enjoy the offerings of their five star Hotel before finally returning to London.

His thoughts lazily returned to the present to Rebecca. How easily everything had fallen into place with David and Rebecca finally joining in wedlock. Two separate families as a dynasty, so to speak. How events had shaped themselves was really unimaginable good luck. Well not quite! Cynthia had been instrumental in bringing them together. The woman was a marvel, a treasure, and in his own way he loved, or at least, was very fond of her. As for the age difference that was a minor factor but since his honeymoon he had put on a little weight and narcissistic as he was, insisted he was looking older for it!

The sound of Cynthia entering the room interrupted his reverie. 'Is there anything you would like me to do darling?' Cynthia asked. 'No, my dear, I was just thinking about David and Rebecca and remembering the wonderful time we spent together on our honeymoon!' Cynthia's face flushed with happiness. 'Yes it was a wonderful time. I only hope David and Rebecca have as much fun as we experienced together!' 'Has David told you where he is taking Rebecca after the wedding?' Robert asked. 'No not as yet. He desperately wants to keep it as a surprise and is quite paranoid that one of us will spill the beans. I assured him, or tried to, that we of all people would be able to keep something as important as that, under our hats, but the poor man is certain that it will get out somehow or other!' Robert nodded. He knew how fraught these times could be. Hadn't he sufficient experience himself! Uncomfortable with his memories, he rose from his chair, walking towards the partially covered window. 'So much has happened Cynthia in the last couple of months, it really is remarkable!' Cynthia smiled a warm suffusing smile. 'Yes it is remarkable, but let's not count our blessings too much. We don't want to tempt the devil, do we?'

Chapter 39

'My word she's like a new person. It's given her a new lease of life' Molly prattled on. Arthur sat solidly at the large wooden table, his heavy horn rimmed glasses perched precariously at the end of his nose whilst studying the horse fixtures for the day. Not that he was a gambling man, but the occasional flutter here and there, he told himself, wasn't going to harm anyone. He liked to sit quietly over a pint, now and there, but as far as vices were concerned, he reckoned he was a clean living man. Always had been! Today he was feeling a little irritated. Whenever he tried to relax and not think about anything in particular, Molly would come up with more prattle. 'If only the woman would be quiet for once' he muttered to himself. 'Who?' he mumbled, half listening. 'Once this wedding's over, perhaps we'll have some peace!' 'What's wrong with you?' Molly berated him. 'Surely a little excitement is something to be welcomed?'. He returned her enquiring stare 'Yes, you'll be right there my girl, but enough is enough and I for one won't be sorry to be back in the old way of things!' 'My word you are getting long in the tooth' Molly laughed. 'Whoever would have thought that you would be feeling like this and at your age too?' 'What's age got to do with it?' Arthur replied defensively. 'Men like to be left alone now and then. We are not that interested in local gossip. We leave that to the women folk.' Molly looked at him in total disbelief. 'How can you be calling this local gossip? And how can you be calling anything that's happening under this very same roof local gossip?' Arthur was about to answer when the sound of Anne's gentle knock before entering the kitchen curtailed any further conversation. Anne's face was a picture of happiness which did not go unnoticed. 'You know how Rebecca feels about you attending the wedding' she remarked casting her glance at Molly then Arthur respectively. 'All the arrangements have been made and you'll both be travelling to London with me.' 'That'll be nice,' Molly enthused. 'We'll really be looking forward to that, and a little sad.' 'I'm trying not to feel sad' Anne continued pushing away any feelings of loneliness that she might have contemplated for the future. 'It's really wonderful that Rebecca and David make such a perfect couple. I couldn't have wished for anything more!'

'You see' Molly tried to engage Arthur in conversation once more now that Anne had left the room. 'Look how wonderful Miss Henderson's looks! It's a treat to seeing her look so happy and her being so relaxed.'

Chapter 40

ANNE LITERALLY FLOPPED into her chair facing the patio. Rain was in the air and slight drops were already beginning to settle on the French windows which were partially opened to allow the smooth breeze to waft through. The air felt good, clean and fresh and the birds twittering their songs as dusk began to fall was as pleasant a sound as any to accommodate her mood of well-being. She gazed out at the well-manicured lawn of green, sighing, a sigh of contentment and relief. Rebecca, her daughter, was about to be married to a likeable and upstanding young man, a reliable man of adequate means. No gold hunter, no unestablished young man trying to make his way up the ladder. No, a man who had proved his maturity and was able to provide for Rebecca with a lovely home and everything she could wish for. This pleased Anne greatly. She had heard so many stories of men conning their wives. Hadn't she seen it herself with her sister Sarah and Robert! And David was a divorcee but by no means due to philandering ways. His marriage hadn't worked and although Anne had seen fit to be disconcerted by this news, upon speaking with him he had been able to put her mind at rest in this respect. A Veterinary Surgeon's wife did have a great deal to put up with, but there again so did a vast majority of wives whose husbands had demanding careers. Anne's thoughts wandered off into the past. Sarah was with her now. 'Come on, come on' she would taunt. 'You're so awfully slow!' 'Why can't you walk faster, why can't you.....' Anne began to cry. 'My goodness aren't we the cry baby. Aren't we Mummy's little darling, aren't we,' Anne raised her hands to her eyes. 'Sniffle, sniffle, piffle, piffle, cry and cry and cry. One day when you are older, you'll be crying till you die!' 'That's cruel' Anne retorted. 'Why are you so horrid to me?' Sarah's face lined with pain stared back at her now. 'Oh Sarah, why did we have to fight so much? Life was too short for you. You should have been here now to laugh, share and enjoy! You did all you could possibly have done and I thank you for that from the bottom of my heart. If only you knew the gratitude that I feel and the joy. How much I wish you could be here to see for yourself.'

Rebecca tiptoed into the room unobserved by her Aunt. She stood behind her wondering what thoughts were going on in her mind. 'Should I ask her?' Rebecca was tempted. 'Should I tell her what Mark told me? Tell her how much I am hurting inside, the pain, the anguish, the uncertainty and to what purpose? Even if it were not true I could never convince Mark. Never have him hold me in his strong loving arms. Never know again the warmth of his kisses, the touch of his hands and the feel of his body next to mine. This is the end, not the beginning. No-one would ever understand.

'Rebecca' Anne startled at the slight sound behind her. 'I didn't hear you come in!' 'No Aunt Anne. I came in quietly as you appeared to be so far away. Is there anything on your mind? You seemed so lost in thought.' 'I was, I must admit. I was thinking about your Mother.' Rebecca continued, 'do you think she would have approved of David? What do you think she would have said?' 'Probably the same way I feel Rebecca. She would have wanted to be with you now to share some of your joy and happiness. Are you feeling a little nervous?' Anne asked. 'It's quite normal for the bride also to have pre-wedding nerves.' 'Yes, I suppose I am. It's also.....' Rebecca hesitated. The sound of the telephone brought the conversation to an abrupt halt. 'I would have asked then' Rebecca thought wryly. 'I was just getting over my nerves and then the interruption.' Anne replaced the receiver back on its cradle. 'What were you about to say?' Anne asked. 'It was nothing. You were right though. I do have butterflies in my stomach and I am nervous.' 'Would you like the doctor to prescribe something for you just to help over the next few days?' 'No!' Rebecca replied somewhat abruptly and then realising how she must have appeared 'No, really not. I'm fine. I'll put my mind to other things and one of them will be to guess where David has chosen for our honeymoon.'

Anne sat quietly in deep thought, once Rebecca had left the room. There was something troubling Rebecca but she didn't quite understand what it could be. She should be so happy, so radiant and full of the joys of spring but she was not! It was as if she was worry or confused, uncertain about everything. Yes, even despondent. Perhaps I am reading too much into it, Anne thought to herself. 'Perhaps we are all a little uncertain as to what the future will hold!'

Chapter 41

LIFE WAS STRANGE, an adventure, a weaving together of so many circumstances until they formed a picture. But the picture could never be completed until? Rebecca had lain awake for hours. Hours in which she had pondered the whys and wherefores, the 'ifs and buts', until utterly exhausted, she had fallen asleep only to confront even more nightmares of an imaginary kind. Why, she had asked herself, did it have to be this way. But however hard she tried, she could find no answers to her confused thoughts. By morning she had resolved more or less what she was about to do.

The Harley Street gynaecologist watched her closely as she related her story. He was a kind, sympathetic man used to listening and dealing with women's' problems, so much so that his own and his families problems were always prone to take second place. He listened intently as Rebecca sometimes falteringly explained the circumstances surrounding her pregnancy and the reason for her visit. Obviously she was somewhat emotional, he thought, as he quietly and unobtrusively scribbled some notes on a pad resting on the desk in front of him. 'I think I should examine you now' he added gently. Rebecca undressed behind the screen at the far end of the surgery assisted by a young lady nurse. 'Don't be nervous' she said, having noticed Rebecca's unease. 'He's a lovely man!' Rebecca smiled weakly. Yes she was nervous, very nervous at the thought of being prodded and probed by a complete stranger. Once disrobed, she covered herself with the white gown which the nurse had handed to her. She clambered onto the examining bed waiting for the doctor to appear from behind the flimsy curtain which served as a partition from the office. 'Good' the doctor remarked on pulling back the temporary screen. Slowly and methodically he examined Rebecca. She winced as his fingers probed inside her. It were as if she was being violated and the thought made her shudder. 'It won't take much longer' he reassured her, 'but you are doing very well'. Sliding off the narrow bed she quickly dressed before returning to his desk. He looked up from his notes, slowly, purposefully and then addressed Rebecca in a direct manner. 'If what you say is the correct information' he began, 'then I would possibly suggest a termination. On the other hand, you must realise there is also the possibility that there will be nothing wrong with the unborn child. There are tests that can be undertaken once you reach the three month stage of the pregnancy but these tests in themselves could cause the foetus to abort.' He paused for a moment, 'But, and here I must add that the final decision must be of your making, but under the given circumstances I must admit that I would agree to a termination.' 'What worries me however' he continued, 'is the fact that you seem to be in doubt regarding the true details surrounding the pregnancy and also the fact that you are already deeply and emotionally attached to your unborn child even at such an early stage of its embryonic development.' He paused again as if gathering his thoughts. 'Here I would suggest' he hesitated, 'it may be necessary for me to have you see a colleague of mine who would be more able to assess your mental state before I could continue further.'

Rebecca stared at the doctor, a look of alarm covering her face. 'Are you suggesting that I'm unstable and unable to determine what I should do for myself?' 'Not at all' he cajoled, 'only with my experience we have seen in some instances, and here I must repeat, a few instances, where after the termination has taken place, the person in question has had to receive psychiatric treatment. As responsible doctors in our profession, we now have to evaluate what in our opinion is best for the patient. That is why I hesitate in agreeing at this point in time to make the final decision of an immediate termination.' Rebecca sat quite still trying to digest his words. 'What about the time factor?' she asked. 'Yes, I have given that thought obviously' he replied. 'From my calculations and also what you have given me to understand, I would say you are in your eighth week which is, as you will appreciate, moving on in the pregnancy. I have carried out terminations over twelve weeks and you appear to be quite healthy and fit. I do not foresee any problems whatsoever. You do realise, of course, that this is a highly sensitive matter and you or your next of kin will have to sign various forms before I can continue.' Rebecca nodded. 'There will be no-one with me and I shall be signing the papers myself.' The doctor leaned back in his chair. 'You also realise that should I be prepared to follow this through, the cost will not be small. Monies involved will go to the Anaesthetist, nurses and your one night stay in our private nursing home. There will also be a fee for the Psychiatric report'. 'That won't be a problem' Rebecca responded. 'I will write you a cheque now for today's consultation and another, once the date has been finalised. You do appreciate' she continued in a much quieter and guarded tone, 'that this is highly confidential and not to be discussed with anyone!' 'Of course' the doctor concluded. 'I also for many reasons do not wish it to be known. There are many who do not, or should I say, oppose any such actions so I would ask the same of yourself, or rather, demand the same as yourself should you wish to continue.' Rebecca fumbled in her bag whilst he made a discreet call. 'Can you manage to be at this address' he handed her a piece of paper on which he had written various details, 'by 3:00 p.m. this afternoon? Rebecca studied the paper carefully. 'Yes, I will be there'. 'Good' the doctor replied, shaking her hand, 'and perhaps you will call me at 1:00 p.m. tomorrow by which time I will have your evaluation in hand and also I will be able to tell you exactly how we are going to proceed.'

Rebecca lay awake, unable to sleep, the quiet and darkness of night distorting her thoughts. Night was a good time to think, to reflect, but somehow night brought with it confused ideas and emotions blown out of all proportion. Morning would bring a clearer perspective. Such was the night for Rebecca and as she opened her still sleep filled eyes, so her thoughts became clearer.

'Aunt Anne' she spoke her name hesitantly, knowing the turmoil and havoc she was about to cause. 'Aunt Anne' she repeated, 'I don't want you to worry about me!' She knew her Aunt was perplexed, wondering what was happening and why her niece was calling from somewhere outside. 'I owe it to you' Rebecca confided, 'to explain that I cannot go through with the wedding!' Rebecca waited as Anne took in a deep gulp of air. 'What do you mean Rebecca?' she asked, momentarily stunned by what she was hearing. 'I know this will be hard for you' Rebecca continued, 'but I just can't marry David. I cannot go through with the sham of a marriage when I am not deeply in love with the man I am about to wed!' Rebecca paused. 'That is why I am calling to tell you Aunt Anne. This is so very difficult for me especially when so many people will be hurt in the process. But they would only be hurt later'. She paused again. 'I have given it a great deal of thought. I have lain awake with nights of thinking and asking. You must understand that I never ever wanted to hurt you or anyone for that matter!' Anne waited a moment before responding. 'Are you sure this is what you really want? Are you sure you are not suffering from pre-wedding nerves and that later you will realise it was only that?' 'No Aunt Anne. Believe me please! I know what I am doing, why I am doing it and honestly nerves have no part in my decision.' 'I never realised you were unhappy' Anne continued. 'Why didn't you talk to me? Why didn't you say something? We could have discussed it quietly, everything!' 'I couldn't' Rebecca replied honestly. 'I did try but I couldn't! I promise, once this is all over and the situation quietened down, I promise to be back to talk. I promise you that.' 'What are you saying?' Anne interrupted. 'Are you saying you are not coming home?' 'Not for a while' Rebecca answered sadly. 'Please believe me it's all for the best! Don't worry Aunt Anne. That's one promise you must make to me!' 'That is easier said than done' Anne replied.

Rebecca replaced the phone back in its cradle. As if carried along by some unknown presence, she sat down to write a letter to David. She wanted to explain as much as she could and this was a daunting prospect. Obviously she had to tell him about the child. The child she was carrying not being his. This would be a terrible blow to him but by the time he had read the letter he would feel relieved and well rid of her. Feelings of remorse swamped her as she began to write. This was cowardly, she told herself, but more cowardly would be to lead David along and for him to believe and have faith in her when the circumstances were false. This was the hardest moment she had ever had to experience in her life, for the moment anyway and she was desperately upset that through her own selfishness so many people were about to suffer. She pressed her hands to her throbbing temples. Feeling dizzy and nauseous she hurried to the bathroom and splashed her face with cold water before retching into the toilet bowl. 'Pregnancy at its earliest, the most daunting' she thought, 'but for the majority, well worth it in the end!' It was difficult for her to equate all the events which had led up to this moment in time. How her world had been pulled apart and now, total disarray. If there was an ending to it all, she would like to know when!

Chapter 42

ANNE WAS DEVASTATED. She could not believe what she had just been told. 'It was all a bad dream' she told herself. 'None of this could possibly be happening'. But it was and there was no point going over and over the same questions, the same answers, round and round in circles. Her thoughts turned to David. Poor David, how shocked he would be and how the poor man would feel. All those jokes about the bride being jilted on her wedding day! So chauvinistic, men could be jilted too. But there was no point in brooding over such issues now. There were so many other matters that required attention.

Anne called the Savoy and having spoken to the Banqueting Manager left the matter for his attention. The guest list was a further item to be tackled as she methodically sorted out the various relatives and friends to advise that the wedding would no longer be taking place. Many gifts had also arrived but Anne pushed any thoughts of handling those to one side. Next was the Registry Office. David should take charge of that. It was a perplexing situation and not a pleasant one with so many matters to attend to. The next part was going to be the worst. Rebecca's Father, the man she herself disliked so much who had wormed his way into Rebecca's heart. How would he react to the news? Filled with a certain feeling of trepidation she dialled the London number. Upon hearing the light crisp voice of Lady Cynthia, Anne heaved a sigh of relief. 'Lady Cynthia, it's Anne Henderson'. 'Yes Anne. How pleasant to hear from you!' Not that pleasant Anne thought bracing herself before conveying the bad tidings. 'Is Robert there?' she asked, impatient now for the call to be over and done with. 'No Anne. He won't be home until this evening.' Anne swallowed hard wondering what she should do next. 'Is there anything wrong?' Cynthia asked as if sensing Anne's apprehension. 'Yes' Anne replied falteringly, 'but I suggest you sit down before I give you the news.' Anne hesitated before continuing. 'It concerns Rebecca'. 'Is she all right?' Lady Cynthia interrupted. 'She hasn't been in an accident?' Cynthia sounded alarmed. 'No, no, nothing at all but well, I don't know how to say this, but I must. She's not going through with the wedding!' Anne waited for the stunned silence to end and for Lady Cynthia to take in the enormity of what she had just heard. 'Anne, this can't be possible! This can't be true!' she exclaimed. 'It is' Anne replied. 'Rebecca telephoned me this morning.' 'What do you mean she telephoned you?' 'She's not here' Anne continued. 'She's not at home and didn't stay here last night. She told me, more or less, that she would like time to herself. She's dreadfully upset and I can understand!' Cynthia sighed 'But what about David? How will he, must he be feeling!' 'I don't know' Anne replied. 'Please Cynthia, this is just as upsetting for me, believe me. I take no delight in the news, none whatsoever!' 'Did you try to talk to Rebecca, to talk some sense into her that it could just be pre-wedding nerves.' 'I wish I could say that were the case, but really I can't. I've spent a lot of time with Rebecca over the years and she isn't the type of person to make a hasty decision. Please understand as I am desperately trying to. It's so dreadful and I offer no excuses. I am only the messenger of bad tidings, not the maker!' 'Thank you Anne' Lady Cynthia replied. 'How perfectly selfish of me to bombard you with so many questions when you yourself must be under so much strain with everything you have to do and cope with.' Anne sighed, 'Not as much by any stretch of the imagination as poor David and Rebecca.' 'I'll ask Robert to call you the minute I make contact with him.' 'Thank you' Anne replied. 'I am so sorry that all this has come about.'

Cynthia poured herself a small brandy from the cut crystal glass decanter which rested on the nearby table her hands trembling. 'My poor darling David' she murmured to herself. 'Why did it have to happen to you of all people? You don't deserve this, my poor darling man!'

Chapter 43

DAVID WAS AT the surgery when his assistant brought in the brown envelope delivered by courier marked 'Strictly Private and Confidential.' 'What's this?' he chided as he sat down at his cluttered desk. He carefully removed the contents of the envelope.

'My Dearest David' the letter began. For a brief moment he felt a great apprehension before reading on. 'I realise this will come as a great shock to you, but please try and understand that it is all for the best. Firstly I will tell you some of the circumstances which have forced me to make this decision, the decision, David, not to go through with our wedding vows. David, I know this has shocked you and your thoughts are probably dreadfully confused at this very moment in time and it will be difficult for you to comprehend all I am trying to say. It may be easier if I tell you that I lied to you in the past. David I am sorry, truly I am but the child I am carrying is not yours. I could not say that if it were not true. I thought I would, at one point, be able to carry the deception through and you must believe that

I never wanted to hurt you. I still don't. That is why I have decided that our marriage vows would amount to nothing. A complete farce and if you were not the kind of person you are and if I were to be totally selfish and insensitive, then perhaps I would have proceeded with our plans. David, you are such a wonderful person. You are kind, giving and understanding to a fault. But I deceived you and all I can say is I am sorry. Sorry for the hurt, the embarrassment and for everything I am causing you. You have every right to hate me. Hating perhaps is too kind a word. Loathing would be more fitting. But one thing I must say. That is despite everything David, I do care for you. A great deal in fact, but I cannot pretend to love you and for that I must and have decided, to draw a halt to this sham of which I am the perpetrator. Yes David, I hear you ask me how do I know I do not love you. And, as I will be asked by many, could this be pre-wedding nerves. My answer, sadly, is No. Wedding nerves do not enter a situation where one is giving and receiving love. The simple fact that may hurt you but may also clarify the situation is that I still love someone else. No I have no plans to be with him or him with me, and yes, he is the Father of my child. But until such time as my heart is light and I can genuinely love again, I have no intention of marrying anyone.

> Dear David, I am so sorry but I do not
> expect or will not ask for your forgiveness.
> In time, a little understanding perhaps,

> Rebecca'

David's face paled ashen with the shock of what he was trying to comprehend. The wedding was not to be. Rebecca, dear Rebecca, he loved her and what was worse, he still loved her, wanted her desperately despite all she had written.

'I'm out' he mumbled to his assistant. 'You'll have to manage on your own!' Moving hastily from his desk, he grabbed his brown leather jacket from behind the surgery door. 'Will you be back later?' his assistant asked. 'No. I don't know. Just carry on without me.' The door closed abruptly behind him.

David drove his Austin Healey out of town, his thoughts in total confusion. Tight knots seemed to be holding his stomach together and if he could, he would cry. Still numb with shock his thoughts rambled on and on. 'How could she not have trusted me' he reflected. 'Why hadn't she told him of the true parentage of the child? No, he hadn't wanted a child so quickly into their marriage and he had made that obvious from the start and perhaps this was one of the reasons she had fled. Fled from his wanting arms, from all he longed to give, had to give and he loved her. He had loved her from the very beginning and had been enchanted by her femininity, her smile and her natural ways; so much to love, so much to give. She was like a stray waif waiting to be nurtured and he was there for her. He was missing her now, desperately. 'Rebecca' her name came out in a stifled sob, 'I would take you and another's child. It's not important to me. Can't you understand that? Only you can fill my dreams, my desires, and love, only you, my precious darling, only you.'

'I've tried calling David all day' Cynthia worriedly explained to Robert. 'I just don't know what to do. Really I don't and I am so upset. How must David be feeling? He must be absolutely devastated. Oh Robert, what should I do?' 'Honestly Cynthia, having yourself in a state like this is not going to make things any better. You must calm yourself. Yes, I too am worried for both of them but David is a grown mature man and Rebecca only a child!' 'Only a child?' Cynthia gasped, momentarily taken aback. 'David's my son, for God's sake. I love the man. Can't you understand what effect this will have upon him? It was Rebecca's doing not his!' 'She must have her reason. I wouldn't be at all surprised if it isn't just a case of pre-wedding nerves!' 'That doesn't help to clarify the situation' Cynthia responded. 'That's not going to help David, is it?' 'What else did Anne say?' Robert asked gently. 'Why don't you call her? I know that you aren't the best of friends but surely a situation like this would be the time to bury some of your old grudge, at least for a while!' 'Yes my dear, you are right' Robert replied condescendingly. 'Yes, I will call her now. The woman must have also been in total chaos at the news and my Lord with all the arrangements to be cancelled and everything else!'

Robert's voice greeted Anne in a somewhat restrained and awkward manner. 'What's all this I have been hearing about Rebecca?' he asked. 'Yes it's true' Anne replied. 'She called this morning sounding very upset but definite! 'Do you think it could be wedding nerves?' Robert asked tentatively, 'After all she is quite a sensitive young lady!' 'No Robert, I wish I could say it was the case. It was obvious from the way she spoke and what she had to say that it was much more than that' 'Where is she?' Robert interrupted, 'I would like to see her to talk it through.' 'She didn't say' Anne answered, 'but she did make it quite clear Robert, that she wants to be left alone for while! 'Did she not give you any reason, any reason at all why she has come to this decision?' 'Once again' Anne replied apologetically, 'she hasn't told or talked to me in depth. She said that would come later. Honestly Robert, if I would have thought there was something we could do, I would tell you.' Robert grunted. 'Well all I can say' he added a little off handily, 'this is a bloody mess. I feel sorry for David. How is that poor bastard going to feel? Jilted at the last minute?' 'Not quite' Anne retorted defensively. 'It's not as if she left him standing at the altar, is it!' 'Bloody well hope not!' Robert cursed. 'I can't believe my daughter would do something like this.' Anne chose to remain silent.

Chapter 44

THE FOLLOWING DAY Rebecca busied herself partly by purchasing the necessary toilet requisites for her overnight stay at the clinic and also by meeting up over a coffee with one of her London based friends. Sally was more than sympathetic to her friend's dilemma. Rebecca had previously confided some of her anxieties and it had come as no surprise when Rebecca had called to say that the wedding was off. They sat in empathy together, Sally not asserting herself as far as conversation was concerned, preferring to give Rebecca the opportunity to examine her doubts and thoughts without interruption. 'Is there anything I can do?' she asked before leaving. 'No, but I appreciate your concern and support' Rebecca replied sincerely. 'Should I need you though, I will call you. I promise!'

She had sat quietly on her own once Sally had left, indulging in a vanilla ice cream with hot chocolate sauce. She had found herself experiencing cravings for various food items in the last two weeks and today she had given in to this one. Her thoughts wandered back to Mark. What he was doing and had he thought about her. Thoughts were painful and she conceded that he didn't want any part of this pregnancy. She felt the stinging of unwanted tears and forced herself to hold them back. It was not good. Not good for her or the baby. The realisation of what she was thinking made her start. Tomorrow there would be no child. Tomorrow it would all be over. Heavy hearted she left the coffee bar and made her way back to the hotel. She was feeling desperately lonely and was tempted to call her Father. No, it was better this way. After tomorrow she would feel stronger, more able to cope with all the demands which now weighed heavily on her shoulders. She knew in her heart she had to speak to David at some point. But then the letter was explanatory and perhaps it was better that she stayed out of David's life for a while; sufficient time for him to get over his hurt. Hopefully to appreciate that it was in his interests too, or was she deluding herself.

A little less apprehensively than that of the previous day, Rebecca sat in the spacious, furnished waiting room of Doctor Grant. He greeted her, personally ushering her into the private confines of his surgery. After rummaging through various notes he slowly turned is attention to her once more. 'How are you feeling today?' he enquired, a note of genuine concern entering his voice. Before she had time to reply, he continued, 'I received the evaluation from the psychiatrist and as I suspected he is not one hundred percent in total agreement. Rebecca felt her body stiffen. This was not something she had anticipated. It had all seemed too easy, the irrelevant questions, the nodding acceptance of her answers. The psychiatrist had been a doddery old man reclining in his overstuffed armchair in a dingy room cluttered with dusty old books and oversized furniture which had seen better days. Doctor Grant cleared his throat. 'Even so' he continued, 'should you still wish and are convinced you would prefer to go ahead, then I will help you!' 'What did the psychiatrist object to?' she asked nervously. 'I made it quite clear that I wanted the pregnancy terminated.' 'Yes' Doctor Grant agreed, 'but he felt that your bond with the unborn child was greater than you could possibly realise and that later you may have many regrets.' Rebecca sat quietly taking in the Doctor's words. 'Yet you are still prepared to help me despite that?' 'In this instance, yes Rebecca. But now I require your confirmation that it is what you want to do!' Rebecca breathed a sigh of relief. 'Would the day after tomorrow be suitable?' He paused, 'You would need to be at this address by 10:00 a.m.' He handed her a typewritten sheet. 'The procedure will be performed early afternoon and we would require you to spend the night at the clinic and discharged the following morning after I have examined you. Everything you need to know is explained on the information sheet. If you have any questions, there is a number listed which you can call at any time.' Rebecca nodded agreement. Finally she felt her worries would be over and then her normal life would return.

Feelings of elation engulfed her on the journey back to her hotel, but these gradually dissipated giving way to feelings of despondency, a void, deep sinking feeling in the pit of her stomach. Once more the strains of the pregnancy and everything which had taken place were making themselves felt.

Chapter 45

THE FLICKERING CANDLELIGHT danced in the darkness as Rebecca sat quietly on the veranda in the warm night air. A cool breeze funnelled the slightly humid atmosphere whilst the gentle sound of the waves lapping against the shore, lulled her thoughts. Here she was at peace, alone yet not alone, undaunted by her singular existence.

Looking downwards she could make out the inky blackness of the ocean. The moon was not yet full. A few more nights and it would bring in its wake stronger winds and perhaps some squally showers. The moon appeared to govern so many aspects of one's life here. By day the skies were mostly blue with fluffs of white clouds, like puffed up marshmallows, dotting the horizon. The ocean would magically transform from inky blackness into hues of turquoise and greens edged with golden sands laced with swaying palms and coconut trees. Along the shore fishermen would clean and sort their catch, patiently awaiting the villagers armed with tin buckets or plastic bowls, to make their daily purchases. And on a good day, the fishermen's faces, parched and aged by the sun and sea would be wreathed in smiles as they gossiped after their hard night's work. Tourists would watch and sometimes help them in the laborious task of hauling in their now heavily laden nets of fish, crabs and other crustaceans. The coarse ropes would rub against the soft flesh of their hands, unaccustomed to this daily ritual and the fishermen would smile knowingly. Dogs or pot-bellied hounds (as the locals called them) would hover nearby in eager anticipation of a meal of raw fish which would spill over from the laden nets onto the warming sand. But there were mornings when the fishermen were not to be seen. Rough seas had little regard for their needs. Small boats were buffeted by the strong waves and the gulls and pelicans normally hovering overhead, were nowhere to be seen.

Rebecca watched a frog as it hesitated on the grass verge in front of her. They always ventured forth as night descended, their familiar croaks reminding her of younger years. Two Night Jars fluttered alternately overhead, the light from the spluttering candle providing easy unsuspecting insects of prey. In the distance she could hear the muted sounds of pan being played inviting all to 'wine' and dance.

This was the Caribbean, the island of Tobago, comparatively unknown to the outside world but a place where she had run in her desire to escape, to find refuge. How traumatic it had been at the time and now she was no longer plagued by doubts. No longer was she afraid of the unknown. Here she was at one with herself, her thoughts and her very existence.

Her mind wandered back to London, to the Clinic where she had filled in seemingly endless forms and the waiting in a hushed atmosphere where one could sense the heightened feelings of apprehension. It all seemed so very far away! 'How are you?' Doctor Grant had asked in his matter of fact but sympathetic manner. And somehow he had touched a nerve as the deluge of tears flowed unceasingly down her cheeks. 'Now, now' he had comforted her, 'it's not too late!' And she had stared at him, her face flushed from crying, trembling in anticipation as to what she was about to say. 'I can't go through with it!' she had stammered. 'I'm so dreadfully sorry but I can't go through it with.' More tears had flowed but he had been understanding and kind. 'Don't worry my dear' he had tried to reassure her. 'I somehow knew you wouldn't. This comes as no surprise to me at all. It was just a matter of time for you to acknowledge your own feelings.' He nodded his head knowingly, 'Just a matter of time.'

A slight stirring in her belly brought her back to the present. It hadn't been that difficult to organise her flight and she had been early enough in her pregnancy to travel. On arriving at Piarco Airport in Port of Spain, she had flown in a small aircraft and landed at a makeshift landing strip on the island of Tobago. Robinson Crusoe Island, the Captain of the aircraft had told her later. He had taken her to a small boarding house not too far away and had later helped her find a small house perched on a cliff overlooking the ocean. This was now her rented home and in Stephen Lamming she had found a friend and she was grateful for that. He was a Trinidadian by birth, slim, of medium height, slightly dark of skin with curly black hair flecked with grey which served to show his Negroid ancestry. His appearance suggested a man in his late forties and she had gathered during their early conversations that he was unmarried or divorced, but that was his business and she had no reason to pry into his personal affairs.

Once settled she had written to Aunt Anne and her Father reassuring them that she was safe and well. She would be returning home, she had told them, once she had explored these unknown shores and once the feelings to return overcame her. But, at the same time she had omitted to tell them of her pregnancy and in another short note to David, had asked that he respect her confidence. Meanwhile she had assured them she was happy and enjoying the opportunity to experience a different and more uncomplicated way of life.

The villagers had welcomed her with open curiosity, eager to understand why a young woman from far off shores should drift into their world alone. But they did not pry. Their curiosity was never an intrusion. Given time they would learn more about her but meanwhile she was their friend and they, hers. Again she felt a slight movement in her stomach. 'My baby is impatient to greet the world' she murmured, but it was much too early!

A strange light caught her eye and then another as it edged its way along the beach its luminous glow playing tricks in the dark. Once more the poachers were on the prowl for this was the season for the turtles, March to August their nesting time. But these were no ordinary species. These were the Giant Female Leatherbacks with some weighing up to 728 kilograms with carapace lengths of approximately 125 to 185 cm returning to their place of birth to lay their eggs. And each turtle would lay between 80 and 125 white eggs, the shape of miniature golf balls at one time. Rebecca had watched incredulously as the turtle had laboriously made its way on to the dry shore and then, with her large giant flippers, excavated the sand. Slowly she had deposited her eggs, her eyes coated with heavy mucus, giving the impression of tears. Once her eggs were laid she had then covered them with sand before dragging her tired body back to the ocean. Behind her, covered in a large sandy mound, after an incubation period of fifty to seventy days, the hatchlings would emerge and no bigger than the palm of her hand, escape to the sea. How distressed she had been when walking along the beach to find the mutilated corpses of these wonderful creatures. The fishermen understood her distress. They had explained that there were those who liked to cook the meat and the eggs and how they tenderised it with pawpaw, a local fruit, and brought out the flavour with coconut milk. Tears had come to her eyes as she had pleaded with them to stop the massacre of such sacred animals, but there was nothing they could do. And now the lights were nearer and she could hear the barking of dogs as they sensed an impending kill.

Rebecca rose from her wicker chair and placed the candle inside the house on a small wooden table. Now was not the time to hear the laughter and the noise of man assaulting and defying nature. Now was the time to retreat and in her heart accept that here was an existence even though so very beautiful, alien and primitive to her own.

As night wore on as Rebecca slept, the sound of man and dogs gradually faded. The noise of the Cocoricos, large brown fleshy birds, similar she thought to wood pigeons which the locals also liked to catch and eat, awoke her at dawn, their grating cries seemingly echoing their name. Rebecca turned over in her bed and through the partially closed shutters could see that dawn had broken. She loathed the sound of the Cocoricos. Stephen had chuckled as she tried to imitate their call. 'Honestly Stephen, I cannot think of any other creature that makes such an awful noise!' 'What about the cockerel' he had asked jokingly. 'I really don't think that the cockerel can be likened to the Cocoricos.' Rebecca had replied. 'But you must admit' he added, 'we have the most wonderful profusion of birds here the likes of which you will never see in Europe or England.' She had agreed for the sight of the iridescent Blue-crowned Motmot with its extraordinary racquet-tipped tail, the Rufous-tailed Jacamar with its brilliant plumage of golden green and reddish brown together with a multitude of other bird life, was the most thrilling of experiences. Even the sight of a flock of orange winged green parrots flying way above as she drove with Stephen through the rain forest filled her with amazement, as to see them flying so freely in their natural habitat was one she could never, ever have imagined.

She busied herself preparing breakfast, slicing open a large fleshy pawpaw, part of which she cut into small chunky cubes to which she added banana, melon and pineapple. All these fruits so abundant and fresh and it was the mango season too! On her walks she would pick them up from the roadside where they had fallen, the trees' branches fully laden with huge like pear drops dangling in the sunshine. As she sat on the veranda two Motmots peered down at her from a nearby tree as if waiting for some rewarding treat. She placed a little sugar on a saucer on the table in front of her and watched as the small Bananaquit, locally known as 'Sucrier' or 'Sugarbird' flitted back and forth. Her eyes drifted downwards to the sea. It was calm today and the fishermen were still far from shore. Friday was her scheduled visit to pre-natal classes at the General Hospital. She had made some friends there including that of another English girl, Judy, married to a local Tobagonian. She had explained to Judy that she did not want to be hospitalised for the birth and in turn, Judy had introduced Rebecca to Sherma, a young Tobagonian woman who lived in a village not far from Rebecca's home. Sherma had been quite surprised on hearing Rebecca's request. 'Why not have the baby delivered in the hospital?' Sherma asked inquisitively. 'Because I want a more natural way of giving birth,' Rebecca had replied.

Sherma greeted Rebecca with a hug later that morning. 'Are you sure you be wanting a midwife?' she asked, in her lilting Tobagonian dialect. 'Yes' Rebecca replied, 'that's really how I want to have my baby.' 'Well' Sherma hesitated, 'there's an old lady in another village not too far away. She delivered many babies here. Would you like to meet she?' 'Yes' Rebecca replied enthusiastically. 'Yes, I would like that very much!' 'You come to me for tea today?' Sherma continued, 'and I see what I can do.' Rebecca knew by now that tea was not at the customary time as in England, but their evening meal.

Sherma's small house was within walking distance, and by late afternoon, before dusk, she made her way along the dirt track side road that led to her home. A black, muscular, well-built man greeted her. 'Sherma say you was coming' he grinned. 'She tell me you interested in the old lady from next village to deliver your child.' Rebecca sipped on some fresh sweet coconut water, which Roy handed her. 'Yes that's true and I really am looking forward to meeting her.' 'Don't you tink' Roy continued, thoughtfully scratching the side of his head, 'don't you tink your first be delivered in the hospital?' 'Not really' Rebecca responded. 'I always thought that I would have my babies this way!' Roy nodded. 'Sherma been preparing all afternoon for your tea.' Sherma interrupted, 'Don't be listening to mans' talk. I was making some pigeon peas and rice with stewed chicken. I hope you like it.' Two small girls hid behind their Mother's back, their large brown eyes mirroring their curiosity. 'This is Palm, she being born on Palm Sunday and this is June' their Mother said proudly. 'We hoping the next be a boy if the Good Lord is willing!' 'I didn't realise you had two children' Rebecca commented. 'You look too young for that!' 'We start young here. We like plenty children. That's no problem here.' Roy grinned. He seemed a good man. 'Business plenty good man! My taxi bring me good business from Arnos Vale and the tipping really good.' Rebecca smiled. Stephen had told her about the various hotels on the island, some of which courted a more expensive way of life. It was especially good for the local taxi drivers with their old American cars which plied between the airport and the hotels around. She was looking forward to visiting them and was glad that she had brought a couple of full length dresses that would serve also to hide her bulging stomach. 'I bring the old lady to see you tomorrow' Sherma interrupted. 'That's such good news' Rebecca replied before settling down to enjoy her meal.

By early evening she was ready to leave and Roy walked her home. 'Thank you Roy' she said firmly gripping his hand, 'I do appreciate all that Sherma is doing for me! The meal was wonderful.'

Chapter 46

THE OLD LADY'S skin was dark and lined, as if all her years had been spent under the sun's incessant glare. Her eyes had lost that sheen and her hair was streaked with grey, its coarseness emphasised by the tightness of its curl. She was thin and old but Rebecca guessed she was far older in her appearance than years. A stick intricately carved from bamboo aided her walk. A simple dress of blue cotton covered her frail frame and on her feet she wore brown leather strap sandals. Her fingers, long and bony, were adorned with silver rings and around her neck she wore a cross of shiny black coral.

Sherma stood behind her as they entered. 'What can I get you to drink?' Rebecca asked at the same time drawing three chairs closer together. 'Coconut water' the old lady replied now resting her frail body on one of the chairs. Rebecca nervously poured three glasses from a plastic jug, beads of perspiration covering her brow. It was hot today, particularly hot with no cooling breeze. The humidity was beginning to climb with every passing day and she longed for the luxury of an air conditioned room.

The old lady stared at Rebecca, her eyes unashamedly passing over every inch of her body finally resting on her stomach. 'I have been told you have delivered many, many babies' Rebecca spoke quietly. 'Yes' the old lady nodded. They sat in silence for a while until Rebecca spoke again. 'No doubt Sherma explained to you that I am looking for a midwife to deliver mine!' 'Yes' the old woman replied, 'but first I must feel your stomach and then decide with the Good Lord's blessing nearer the time.' 'How many babies have you delivered?' Rebecca asked. The old lady's face creased into laughter. 'Oh my Lord, Oh my Lord' she cackled. 'I couldn't know that.' And then amused more than ever her face creased into laughter once more. 'Did you train at the hospital?' Rebecca asked once the laughter had faded. 'No, No. Nobody train me but the Good Lord himself. He tells me what to do and I follow his judgement. All is in the hands of Jesus. My darling babies are all in his hands.' 'When will you let me know if you will deliver my baby?' Rebecca asked. 'All in the hands of Jesus.' the old lady repeated looking upwards to the sky. 'But I need to know!' Rebecca pleaded. 'I have to make arrangements.' The old lady stared vacantly ahead. Rebecca sighed. 'So when do I need to see you again?' she asked. The old lady stared back at her. 'Later, later, then I will know. Not now.' 'Where will I find you?' Rebecca pleaded. 'Miss Sherma know where to find me. She tell you when I am ready.' The old lady stood up impatiently tapping her stick on the wooden floor. Sherma placed an encouraging arm around Rebecca's shoulders. 'Don't vex yourself. Have patience.' she whispered in Rebecca's ear.

Chapter 47

STEPHEN POURED HIMSELF a small brandy from a bottle he had brought with him from Trinidad. 'Would you like a drop?' he offered. 'No thanks' Rebecca replied. 'I've decided to stay off the booze until after the baby is born!' Pulling two chairs out on the veranda, they both sat quietly breathing in the night air, grateful for the cool breeze which now accompanied them. 'I saw the midwife today' Rebecca commented, 'Sherma brought her here this morning.' Stephen regarded Rebecca quizzically. 'I thought you were going to have the baby at the hospital?' 'No' Rebecca replied. 'I'm going there for pre-natal classes but I thought I told you that I wanted to have the baby delivered at home.' 'But there can't be many midwives here!' Stephen commented. 'Apparently' Rebecca interrupted, the old lady has delivered many of the babies here.' 'But not for Europeans' Stephen interrupted. 'What difference is there in delivering for a European?' Rebecca exclaimed in astonishment. Stephen's expression was puzzled. 'Well the locals are stronger for one. More resilient

I suppose. That's how I would see it!' 'But there is no difference between white women having a child than a black woman!' Rebecca retorted. 'I'm not a doctor Rebecca' Stephen adamantly continued, 'but I would think it more advisable to give birth to your first child at a hospital than have a midwife delivery. It just seems so much safe, more sensible and practical.' Rebecca shrugged her shoulders non-committedly. 'She hasn't said she will deliver it for me. The old lady has to make up her mind later.' 'How much later?' Stephen asked, a note of disbelief tempering his voice. 'I don't know exactly' Rebecca replied defensively not wishing to tell him the old lady's exact words. 'Well, it's your decision Rebecca. Remember that if you are worried or need a specialist, I can always put you in touch with the right people in Port of Spain. I must confess I've not had any experience with doctors or midwives here.' 'You are such a good friend Stephen! I was so lucky to meet you!' Stephen grinned, momentarily basking in the flattery. 'It works both ways you know.' he replied. 'Now why don't I go and get us some crab and dumpling?' 'That would be wonderful' Rebecca agreed enthusiastically. 'But please let me come with you!' She hurriedly gathered her bag and applied some fresh lipstick before clambering into Stephen's jeep. It was good to get out for a while. To take in the sound of Bucco where the locals and tourists would lime and dance to the latest rap music and yes, she was hungry, but once more her yearning was for vanilla ice cream and hot chocolate sauce. She made a mental note to buy some chocolate in the supermarket and also to remind Stephen the next time he was flying to Port of Spain to look for some special chocolate there. Certain items of food were much more easily obtained in Trinidad than Tobago and she realised she would have to make a list as she could not expect Stephen to remember them all.

Chapter 48

TIME WAS PASSING slowly in her now familiar surroundings. Cocooned in her anonymity she was never questioned as to her past. This was how she wanted it to be leading up the birth of her child. Mark's child!

The light cast strange shadows around her and she could hear the constant ebb and flow of the ocean crashing down over the rocks on to the flat, hard sand, harsher tonight due to the approaching full moon. In another day or two the sea would writhe and squirm, churning up the belly of the ocean floor. Then in more subdued moments, Rebecca would walk along the shore collecting odd shells, chunks of coral and odd pieces of bric-a-brac together with anything unusual that lay in her path. Sometimes she would accompany Susan, and together they would drive in her old battered jeep to the Atlantic side of the island. They would pass through the main town of Scarborough out towards Studley Park via a narrow winding road built into the cliff face overlooking the ocean until they reached a wide open stretch of beach. There they would find sand dollars, creamy white delicate molluscs shaped like irregular stars, and once home she would carefully rinse out the damp sand and leave them to bake and harden under the glare of the sun. Susan would look for gnarled misshapen pieces of wood already bleached white and smoothed by the constant lashing of the sea. Rebecca was always surprised at Susan's finds, her flair for discovering so much in so little. She lived in a small wooden house which she had turned into an art gallery where she also gave lessons to the locals and those who had a desire to paint and work with the coral, wood and anything else of a creative nature. Susan was well known on the island. She had arrived on a carefree holiday leaving her friends and family behind in the U.K. then deciding to start a new chapter of her life in Tobago. There were other women like Susan finding the pace of life much more to their liking and the people kinder and more understanding.

Stephen was in Trinidad and tonight she was content to be alone. For a brief moment she felt a deep ache of despondency. What was Mark thinking now? Had he thought of her? Missed her? Or was he totally oblivious to the pain and anguish which he had caused with his nonsensical words uttered by a dying man! Sometimes the words would go round and round in her head, like an old recording, and as much as she tried, she could not comprehend their meaning.

And David, poor David, the innocent party caught up in her selfish desire to paper over the cracks of her indiscretion. How glad she was that she had taken the difficult path of facing up to the situation by being honest with him. She regretted the distress caused but sometimes it was difficult to do exactly what one would expect of others. Aunt Anne was unaware of her pregnancy and she was quite sure that David would not have broached the matter with any of the family. Jenny had written with news of the shop. There was sufficient stock to carry on for quite some time and she was competent and trustworthy. Rebecca had been able to communicate with her regularly collecting her mail from the tiny make-shift post office, a ten minute walk away. The mail was delivered from Trinidad to the main post office of Tobago in Scarborough. There it was sorted and re-distributed to the small Post Offices dotted across the island. Sometimes she would take the small dusty bus on its long bumpy winding route into the town. A journey which she would not be happy to endure for much longer, preferring the comparative luxury of the crammed conditions of a taxi!

The hustle and bustle of the local people going about their daily tasks reminded her of a world far away. The open stalls of the market adjacent to the main post office were most intriguing with their assortment of provisions. Open shops lined the main and side streets selling clothing, shoes, materials, electrical goods and many other items. The loud sound of rap and pan music permeated the air. Sparrow and many of his contemporaries could be heard singing the latest calypsos. The locals had explained to her how every year at Carnival there would be competitions for the best pan players, calypsos and extravagant costumes. They had told her how exciting and colourful it was and how tourists from other islands came to Trinidad especially to enjoy this spectacular event.

The following day Stephen had planned they drive to the other side of the island to a place called Speyside, well known for diving and snorkelling. Rebecca was looking forward to the drive and also visiting a place she had not seen.

Stephen arrived mid-morning with bottles of mineral water and some snacks. 'We can stop at the Argyle Falls and have a rest there later he suggested. It was a beautiful drive through small villages with many scenic views until they reached the Falls. Gingerly climbing over wet, slippery rocks, they could hear the sound of free cascading water nearby. A couple of tourists accompanied by some local young boys grinned at them as they passed by, eager to venture further within the rocks around the Falls. 'That's one way they can earn some pocket money' Stephen commented. 'It keeps them from becoming bored and gives them an incentive to work and earn their own money!' In the distance they could hear the laughter of the tourists as they scrambled over the slippery ground nearer to the Falls.

Rebecca sat in deep thought. The cool water soothed her aching ankles which had become slightly swollen from the heat. 'Don't get too comfortable' Stephen warned. 'We still have quite a way to go!' A little reluctantly Rebecca followed Stephen back to the jeep.

The pot holed roads were an obstacle to their journey forcing the jeep to slow down. By the time they reached Jemima's Kitchen, a wooden shack with small tables and chairs surrounded by some trees overlooking the winding road, they were both hungry. They tucked into a local dish of black eyed peas, curried crab and dumplings washed down with warm, local beer. 'I really feel I could sleep for a hundred years' Rebecca sighed. Stephen yawned, the effect of the driving and tasty food making him feel sleepy too.

Speyside was everything Rebecca had expected and more! Small chalets lined the beach within a stone's throw from the sea which was now quite rough, topped with peaks of white froth. Several groups of divers were gathered in individual groups waiting to be taken out on small boats for their adventures into the mysteries of the deep waters below. Rebecca watched as they pulled on their black wet suits and checked their equipment. It was a lovely place and she sat down on the welcoming hard sand, gazing out to sea. Stephen joined her and pointed to a small building with an open bar. 'Come on' he coaxed. 'We can sit and have a cold drink. I know the owners. They came here from Trinidad some years ago and decided to stay as they loved it so much. Trinidad is so different from Tobago although driving through the rain forest is something that everyone should do when visiting there.' 'Yes, I would love to do that' Rebecca replied. 'Sherma told me about a place where you can watch the humming birds and also walk into a sort of nature park. It sounded wonderful!' 'Yes' Stephen commented, 'I have been to many nature reserves and enjoyed them immensely. We should plan on doing something like that soon.'

Rebecca was beginning to look more relaxed and well. He had the feeling that she was beginning to understand whatever had been troubling her and hoped that she would be able to sort out any problems that needed to be resolved. He admired her strength of character, her determination to do what she believed in but at the same time felt she needed so much more, something he was unable to provide, apart from his friendship.

Chapter 49

ANNE BUSIED HERSELF with some light chores. Days passed more slowly since Rebecca had left and she had not been in touch with Robert Lawson, preferring to communicate with Lady Cynthia. Molly was bewildered by all the changing of events but had kept her thoughts discreetly to herself.

The phone rang in the small sitting room and on answering Anne was surprised to hear David's voice. 'Aunt Anne' David began, 'I wondered if you had heard anything further from Rebecca?'

He had been absolutely devastated by her actions but still could not stop worrying and thinking about her. 'Oh David' Anne replied, feeling the pain and sadness in his voice. 'I wish I had more news but I really don't' she added. 'Well' David continued, 'I have decided that I have to see her and speak to her!' Anne felt the hairs on her neck stand on end. On one hand she felt absolutely relieved and on the other, a little apprehensive. 'Have you mentioned anything to Robert or your Mother' she asked tentatively. 'No' David replied, 'and I would really ask that we keep this between just us and noone else!' Anne sighed, a deep long sigh of relief and anticipation. The thought that David was making plans to see Rebecca was more than she could ever have wished for. More than that what else could she do? Rebecca could never ever have dreamed how she was feeling. All the worry and sadness had been a nightmare but now David loved Rebecca enough to want to see her and to be with her again. Yes she had heard that Mark was also having so much to cope with since the loss of his Father. His Mother had taken a turn for the worse but hopefully she would gradually return to health and strength. It had all been too much. Mark was not for Rebecca although he loved her with all his heart and soul. Some things were never meant to be and she thought about her parents and Sam. Had the war not intervened who knows! Life was like this, a long winding path of questions but no answers. Only what ifs! 'What if?' she whispered, 'what if!'

Chapter 50

THE SMALL PLANE screeched to a halt on the tarmac. A tall, slim man carrying a small suitcase engaged in conversation with a local man before clambering into his waiting taxi. Roy grinned from ear to ear. 'Yes I take you to Miss Rebecca. She never told Sherma and me you were coming.' David looked around hesitantly. 'It's a surprise, and I hope she will be happy to see me!' Roy smiled. He was relieved that there was someone visiting Miss Rebecca. His wife was worried about her and she could only do so much. As for the midwife, the old lady from the village, he didn't like the idea of Rebecca having her to deliver the baby. The woman had no experience with the likes of she and the thought of anything going wrong was a great responsibility and also a worry.

Roy pulled in to a small clearing and pointed to the small shack, half hidden by the trees. 'This is her home' he pointed, refusing to accept any money for the ride. 'This be my card,' he added, placing his business card in David's outstretched hand.

David waited for the taxi to disappear before walking to the entrance of the small shack. It was quiet as he sat down on the chair overlooking the beach and ocean. It felt good to be in the warmth and fresh sea air. It had been a long flight but he had stayed overnight near the Airport in Trinidad before catching the small plane to Tobago. Anne had given him sufficient information and in a small place like Tobago, news and gossip travelled fast. He had been very fortunate to meet Roy at the Airport. That was a stroke of luck. He hoped his meeting with Rebecca would prove just as happy and she would understand why he had come.

Rebecca had been quietly lying on her bed when she heard the noise of a car drawing to a halt outside. Since her visit to Speyside with Stephen she had found herself thinking more deeply about 'her world' and everything that had happened leading up to where she was now. She had thought a great deal about everyone whose lives had been affected by her actions and also about Aunt Anne. Perhaps she had been too hard on David. How could anyone have possibly foreseen what was to happen. How she could have met up with Mark, so very much younger than his Father and also still living in the village. She missed Roynick and her way of life. She missed Mark but also David. Somehow she felt that she had not yet fitted all the pieces together but no matter what, she was going to have Mark's child irrespective of the consequences.

A light tapping on the door brought her back to earlier thoughts. 'I won't be a moment' she called, tidying her hair and covering her bare shoulders with a light cotton shawl before walking out onto the small balcony.

Chapter 51

DAVID PREPARED THE details for the flight back to London. It had been a long week in which he had listened to Rebecca's story and spent time with her exploring the island. Yes, she had been shocked and surprised to see him standing there but at the same time understanding and happy. He had met up with Stephen and Sherma and other local Tobagonians nearby. They were all so friendly and delighted to meet him being a friend of Rebecca. Stephen had explained how he had met Rebecca and how they had become friends. Also his concerns regarding Rebecca's decision to have the baby at home instead of using the local hospital. David listened intently making comments when necessary. He thanked Stephen sincerely for all his concerns and the two men enjoyed their time together sharing many experiences over a glass or two of the local brew and exchanged contact details for the future promising to be in touch.

As the flight chugged down the runway, David reflected on everything that had happened over the last weeks. It had been a difficult time but now he was on his journey home. He was relieved that he had made the trip to Tobago. Happy and relieved that he had now come to terms with the past and the future. He was looking forward to seeing his Mother, and Aunt Anne, not forgetting Rebecca's Father. They would all be anxious to hear all the news relating to his visit. He was anxious for them to finally understand that all was well and there was no need for them to worry. Rebecca was safe and in good health.

He looked out of the small window as the plane gradually soared higher and higher. 'Are you happy?' he asked tentatively, caressing Rebecca's hand. 'Yes' she replied. 'Very. Now we are going home!'

THE END

Printed in the United States
By Bookmasters